"Don't move."

Caroline heard Henry's voice clearly, but he was too far back to step in before the wolf attacked. Biting her lip to keep it from shaking, she stared at the wolf's long face. He waved his bushy tail and watched her.

"Easy, boy." Henry's voice was closer now, but Caroline was still terrified. Clenching her fists, she closed her eyes so tightly it hurt.

"Easy, boy." Henry's voice was right behind her now, but Caroline still couldn't move. It wasn't until she felt a sticky tongue on her fingers that she finally opened her eyes. Standing right beside her, his tail wagging, the wolf was licking her fingers.

BE SURE TO READ OTHER BOOKS IN
THE LITTLE HOUSE FAMILY

The Martha Years
Laura's great-grandmother, born 1782
LITTLE HOUSE IN THE HIGHLANDS
THE FAR SIDE OF THE LOCH

The Charlotte Years
Laura's grandmother, born 1809
LITTLE HOUSE BY BOSTON BAY
ON TIDE MILL LANE

The Caroline Years
Laura's mother, born 1839
LITTLE HOUSE IN BROOKFIELD
LITTLE TOWN AT THE CROSSROADS

The Laura Years
America's Original Pioneer Girl, born 1867
LITTLE HOUSE IN THE BIG WOODS
FARMER BOY
LITTLE HOUSE ON THE PRAIRIE
ON THE BANKS OF PLUM CREEK
BY THE SHORES OF SILVER LAKE
THE LONG WINTER

LITTLE TOWN ON THE PRAIRIE
THESE HAPPY GOLDEN YEARS
THE FIRST FOUR YEARS

By Cynthia Rylant:
OLD TOWN IN THE GREEN GROVES
Laura Ingalls Wilder's
Lost Little House Years

The Rose Years
Laura's daughter, born 1886
LITTLE HOUSE ON ROCKY RIDGE
LITTLE FARM IN THE OZARKS

ADDITIONAL LITTLE HOUSE BOOKS
NELLIE OLESON MEETS LAURA INGALLS

LITTLE TOWN
AT THE CROSSROADS

by **MARIA D. WILKES**

HarperTrophy®
An Imprint of HarperCollins*Publishers*

To my mother and father,
whose loving home I
return to again and again,
in thought, in spirit, and in heart.

Harper Trophy®, ▪®, Little House®, and The Caroline Years™
are trademarks of HarperCollins Publishers.

Little Town at the Crossroads
Copyright © 2007 by HarperCollins Publishers
www.littlehousebooks.com

Library of Congress Cataloging-in-Publication Data
Wilkes, Maria D.
    Little Town at the crossroads / Maria D. Wilkes. — Abridged
HarperTrophy ed.
        p. cm.
    Summary: An abridged version of the story of young Caroline Quiner,
who would grow up to become Laura Ingalls Wilder's mother, as she and her
family have new adventures as the frontier outpost of Brookfield, Wisconsin,
grows into a bustling town.
    ISBN 978-0-06-114822-4 (pbk.)
    I. Ingalls, Caroline Lake Quiner—Juvenile Fiction. [1. Ingalls, Caroline
Lake Quiner—Fiction. 2. Wilder, Laura Ingalls 1867–1957—Family—
Fiction. 3. Frontier and pioneer life—Wisconsin—Fiction. 4. Wisconsin—
Fiction. 5. Family life—Wisconsin—Fiction.] I. Title.
PZ7.W648389Lk 2007   2007011855
[Fic]—dc22   CIP
                                                                     AC

Typography by Christopher Stengel
❖
First Harper Trophy Edition, 1997
Abridged Harper Trophy Edition, 2007

CONTENTS

LITTLE TOWN AT THE CROSSROADS

FLAGS AND FIFES

"If we don't hurry, Eliza, we're going to miss everything!" Caroline said, pulling her little sister's hand.

"The Glorious Fourth has barely begun!" Mother said. "Don't worry. We'll not miss the parade."

Brookfield was perfectly suited to greet the Glorious Fourth. Every road bustled with townsfolk dressed in their Sunday best heading to the crossroads of town to celebrate Independence Day. All five Quiner children's eyes grew wide as they took in the festivities, but Caroline thought she was the most excited.

This was her favorite holiday.

"Caroline and Martha, I need you to keep hold of Eliza and Thomas," Mother said, handing the babies to Caroline and her older sister. "As for you boys, Joseph and Henry-O, let's find a place for you to set down those picnic baskets. Mother Quiner, where would you like to sit?"

As Grandma scanned the crowded square, a loud noise right behind them made the whole family jump. *Zzzsss, pop! Zzzsss, bang!*

Grabbing Eliza, Caroline dashed to the side of the road as three sizzling firecrackers wriggled past and popped with a quick flip and tumble on the bumpy road ahead.

"No need to practice your jig 'fore tonight, little Brownbraid." Henry laughed out loud. "Those firecrackers won't hurt anybody."

From behind them, a friendly voice boomed almost as loud as the firecrackers. "Good morning, neighbors!"

Mr. Benjamin Carpenter was dressed in his finest Sunday suit. A brown beard covered his chin, and his long, thick brown hair was neatly combed and smoothed behind his ears.

"Can't recollect a prettier day for the Glorious Fourth. How 'bout you, little Brownbraid?" Mr. Carpenter asked Caroline.

"No, sir." Caroline was only seven years old, and she couldn't remember many Fourth of Julys. All she recalled was the wonderful cheering and music.

Benjamin's wife, Sarah, beamed at Caroline, Eliza, and Martha. "You all look very pretty today."

"Thank you, ma'am," Caroline replied bashfully. Standing so close to Mrs. Carpenter, she couldn't help thinking that her own yellow church dress looked anything but pretty. Mrs. Carpenter's long-sleeved dress hugged her waist and ballooned into a wide, round skirt that swayed from side to side as she walked. Caroline looked up at Mother's simple black dress and silently wished that Mother could sometimes wear the beautiful dresses she worked so hard to make for other ladies in Brookfield.

Boom! Boom!

The maple leaves shook as a series of earsplitting blasts pierced the air. Eliza clutched

Caroline's hand. "What was that?" she cried.

"It's just a blast of gunpowder, little one," Mr. Carpenter explained.

"It means we're missing everything!" Caroline cried. "Let's go!"

The road grew even more crowded and noisy as they neared the crossroads of town. Up ahead, a fiddler fiddled and two lanky boys hopped and twirled and kicked their heels together in the air.

A stocky man with twirly whiskers had climbed onto a wide tree stump on the side of the road. "I stand here today, friends," he said, "to remind you it's been seventy years since we freed ourselves from the British! America is the greatest country on earth and we'll fight to keep it free till it's seven *hundred* and seventy years old!"

Caroline felt like shouting, too, but young ladies never shouted if they could help it. She remained quiet, but there was so much to feel proud of today.

When they had set down their picnic next to the Carpenters', Mother told Caroline and

Martha they could find their friend Anna before dinner.

"I bet she's still at the shop with her father," Caroline said, grabbing her sister's hand.

Caroline and Martha wove their way in and out among the townsfolk as they passed the tavern and the blacksmith's shop. All around, people chattered and laughed and greeted their neighbors with warm handshakes and hugs. Young children clung to their mothers' skirts while their older brothers tossed firecrackers and gobbled up handfuls of popcorn and their older sisters swung on tree swings and danced about the square. In front of every building, a cheery flag waved its stars and stripes in celebration.

Finally they arrived in front of the wheel-wright's workshop.

"Hello, Anna!" Caroline called out to her friend as she peered inside the small building that Anna's father shared with the wagon maker. During the day, Joseph Short built cabinets and furniture in the shop. At night, he and Anna lived in the two rooms upstairs.

Anna's brown curls bounced about as she

waved to Caroline and Martha. "Come! You must see what Papa is making!"

Stepping out of the bright sunlight into the dim shop, Caroline and Martha walked carefully around piles of wood, cabinets, tables, and chairs toward the back of the shop. Anna was leaning over her father's workbench as he whittled away at a small piece of wood.

"Look! Papa's making me a fife!" Anna said exuberantly.

"Mornin', Miss Caroline, Miss Martha," Anna's father greeted them in his heavy Scottish burr.

"Good morning, sir," Caroline and Martha answered politely.

Mr. Short pushed a handful of dark curls out of his eyes and glanced over at his daughter. "Be kind and share with your friends, eh, darlin' Anna?"

"Of course, Papa," Anna replied. "Is it finished yet?"

"Try." Mr. Short handed Anna the instrument and watched as she lifted it to her lips.

Anna's cheeks grew even more round and

pink as she blew over the tiny holes as hard as she could. High-pitched squeaks and squeals skirted from one side of the shop to the other.

"It's perfect!" Caroline clapped.

"Blow softer, Anna," Mr. Short suggested. "The sound will be much prettier."

"Yes, Papa," Anna replied happily.

"Come girls, I hear the parade." Mr. Short smiled.

Leading the girls back through the front room, he stood beside the door as they stepped into the brilliant sunshine. Caroline caught her breath as a giant flag marched toward them, a swaying wave of red, white, and blue pointing toward the heavens. A long line of men marched close behind, their trumpets and bugles blasting merrily. Still others followed, tapping, snapping, and booming their drums in response to the bugles' triumphant song.

"There are Henry and Joseph and Charlie!" Martha cried. "There, with the drummers!"

"The fifes and flutes are coming next, Anna." Mr. Short pointed toward the end of the parade, where another group of men, blowing a lilting, joyous melody, was surrounded by children of all sizes, who marched and skipped along. "Go now! You girls should march, too."

So they marched through town, music blaring and flags waving all around them.

> "Hail! Columbia, happy land!
> Hail! Ye heroes, heav'n-born band!
> Who fought and bled in Freedom's cause,
> Let independence be our boast
> Ever mindful what it cost
> Ever grateful for the prize
> Let its altar reach the skies."

Caroline didn't know every word, but she hummed along as best she could. The parade finally passed the crossroads of town, and Caroline saw Mother, Grandma, and the Carpenters on the side of the road, waving as they sang the final refrain:

> "Firm, united, let us be,
> Rallying round our liberty;

As a band of brothers join'd,
Peace and safety we shall find."

As the parade ended, Caroline decided she was very, very glad to be independent and free. If only they could celebrate their freedom more than one day a year!

SPELLING BEE

For days following the Glorious Fourth,
Caroline felt the rush of having marched in
her first parade. She hadn't wanted it to be over,
so she kept marching all around the frame
house, holding an imaginary fife to her lips and
humming "Yankee Doodle." She marched
while she pushed chairs to the table before
every meal, she marched as she carried clean,
dry dishes back to the dish dresser, she marched
while she swept up the bedroom. She marched
swiftly past Joseph and Henry splitting logs
by the woodpile, dodging the stray chunks of
wood spinning through the air. She marched

as she tossed handfuls of oats and corn to the hens scratching and pecking at the dirt around her feet. She marched to school, which got on Martha's nerves, but Charlotte didn't care.

"Will you stop!" her sister said. "You can march again next year in the parade."

But Caroline wouldn't stop. She marched to her bench at school and saluted Anna, who was sitting next to her. She thought she'd march everywhere.

One morning in school, Caroline's teacher, Miss Morgan, called her to the front of the room. "Caroline Quiner," she said. "I'd like you to represent the first primer students today in the spelling bee."

That was enough to stop Caroline in her tracks. Of course, she had studied her spelling words, but never before had she been called to the head of the class. She stood up and hastily smoothed her faded red dress over her petticoats. She smiled thinly at Anna and slowly walked— not marched—to the front of the room.

As she passed the eight rows of benches

packed with girls of all ages and sizes and dotted with a handful of the youngest boys from town, Caroline wished that her stomach would stop flip-flopping. She had recited her spelling words to Mother and Grandma every day for a week. She knew each word by heart, but she was still afraid that she'd forget all her spellings the moment she opened her mouth to recite them in front of the whole class.

Nearing the front of the room, Caroline also began wishing that she had worn her other dress. It wasn't nearly so faded as the one she was wearing. The tiny white dots had practically disappeared into the fabric, and the once-cheerful red color had become a tired pink.

Caroline took her place in line as Miss Morgan looked up and down the rows of benches, searching the room for another first-year student. "Elsa, please come to the front of the room," she finally said.

Standing on her tiptoes, Caroline peered at the back of the room. Elsa Schmidt was seated on the edge of the last bench, her shoulders slumped, her head bowed, and her thick brown hair hanging over her eyes. She didn't look up or move until Miss Morgan called her name again.

"Elsa Schmidt?" Miss Morgan repeated loudly. Elsa's brown eyes looked surprised and uncertain, as though she had heard her name but hoped she was mistaken.

The boy beside Elsa nudged her sideways with his knee until she practically fell off the edge of the bench. As she scuffled to the front of the room her bare feet dragged across the wooden floorboards.

Caroline didn't know whether to be relieved or worried. Elsa had lived in Brookfield for only a month, and she had started school two weeks later than everyone else. Twice, Caroline, Martha, and Anna had asked Elsa to play with them at recess, but both times Elsa had shaken her head and run off without a word. Caroline didn't have any idea how good a speller Elsa Schmidt was, but she had no doubt that Elsa was the most unfriendly girl she had ever met.

"All right, students," Miss Morgan said, "I will give each challenger three words. If you spell a word correctly, you will receive one point. If you do not spell it correctly, I will ask your counterpart on the opposing team to spell the same word. Whichever team first spells the word correctly will be awarded the point. As always, the team with the most points at the end of the spelling bee wins." Miss Morgan smiled at the students who stood nervously waiting to recite their spellings. "Are you ready, scholars?"

"Yes, ma'am," ten voices answered in unison.

"We'll begin with the youngest students today. Caroline, you will go first."

Caroline's heart began pounding so loud, she was certain the first row of students could hear it. Closing her eyes, she concentrated as hard as she could on Miss Morgan's firm but gentle voice.

"The first word is 'mop,' Caroline."

Caroline took a deep breath and, her eyelids still tightly closed, answered in her surest voice, "Mop. M-O-P. Mop."

"That is correct, Caroline. One point for your team," Miss Morgan said. She reached for the slate pencil and scratched a vertical line on one side of the slate.

As Miss Morgan recorded the point, Caroline opened her eyes. Rows of faces were staring up at her intently from the packed benches in the schoolroom. Martha and Anna were sitting up as straight as they could, smiling over all the braided heads in front of them. Martha winked proudly.

"Elsa," Miss Morgan continued, "your word is 'fan.'"

Caroline looked over at the opposite team of spellers and waited for Elsa to begin. Elsa was scrunching the sides of her yellow cotton dress between her fists so tightly, Caroline could see her knuckles turning white. Without lifting her head, Elsa quietly answered, "F-A-N."

"Head up please, Elsa," Miss Morgan said patiently. "I'd like all the students in the classroom to hear your spelling."

The room was silent as Elsa stood stockstill. A tall, freckled girl standing beside Elsa finally squeezed her arm, and Elsa immediately looked back at the schoolteacher.

"Repeat your spelling please, Elsa," Miss Morgan said again.

"F-A-N."

"Correct." Miss Morgan smiled, and scratched a line on the opposite side of her slate.

While the rest of the students in the spelling bee took their turns, Caroline watched Elsa. She wondered what was wrong with her. It was not very nice to refuse to speak to another student, but Caroline couldn't even imagine ignoring a schoolteacher's request.

"We're ready to begin the next round," Miss Morgan said. "Caroline, your word is 'jam.'"

"Jam. J-A-M. Jam," Caroline answered, speaking every letter as clearly as she could.

"Very good," Miss Morgan said, and recorded another point for Caroline's team. "And Elsa, your word is 'sun,' as in 'The sun is shining brightly today.'"

"S . . ." Elsa began, and hesitated for a moment.

"Continue, please," Miss Morgan urged.

"S . . ." Elsa paused again. "U," she said slowly. "N."

"That is correct, Elsa," Miss Morgan said.

It didn't make any sense. Elsa didn't even

follow the spelling-bee rules. She recited letters without stating the word before she spelled it, yet Miss Morgan waited patiently for her answers and praised her responses.

The remaining spellers on each team finished their words, and in no time at all Miss Morgan turned back to Caroline for the final round. Caroline knew that her last word would be the most difficult to spell, so she held her breath and waited for Miss Morgan to speak.

"Your final word is 'nest,' Caroline."

All the fear that had been churning inside disappeared when Caroline heard her last spelling word. She knew it by heart, and she quickly answered, "Nest. N-E-S-T. Nest."

"A fine job, Caroline." Miss Morgan smiled.

"Thank you, ma'am," she said, smiling shyly back at Miss Morgan.

"You are welcome," Miss Morgan replied. After adding Caroline's point to her team's score, she turned to Elsa. "For your final word, Elsa, please spell 'frog.'"

Tiny lines crept across Elsa's forehead "F-R-O . . ." she said, then suddenly stopped.

"Yes, Elsa," Miss Morgan encouraged, "F-R-O . . ."

Elsa pushed her bangs out of her eyes and called out triumphantly, *"Gay!"*

The room was silent. Caroline's eyes stayed fixed on Elsa; strange, unfriendly Elsa who was now making up letters for words she didn't know how to spell.

"I am sorry, Elsa, that is incorrect," Miss Morgan said. Caroline watched as Elsa's blue eyes filled with tears. "If you can spell the word 'frog,' Caroline, your team will receive an extra point."

As her teammates held their breaths, Caroline halfheartedly spelled, "Frog. F-R-O-G. Frog.'"

"That is correct. Your team receives the point, Caroline."

"Nein!" Elsa cried, tears spilling down her cheeks. "Elsa say it! Elsa right!"

"Elsa, there is no such letter as 'gay' in the English language, and the only language we speak in this classroom is English. The correct letter is *g*."

"Nein! Elsa right!" Elsa sucked in breath and

sobs all at once and exclaimed, "Ah-bay-tsay-day-ay-ef-*gay*!" Without another word, she bolted past the packed benches and out the front door of the schoolhouse.

Miss Morgan quickly ended the spelling bee and dismissed the class for dinner. Caroline and Martha walked most of the way home in silence. "You were a real good speller, Caroline," Martha said, pulling open the door.

"Thank you," Caroline answered. But Martha's praise didn't soothe any of the confusion or sadness that Caroline was feeling. For the first time in weeks, she entered the house without marching.

WORDS

Mother wiped her damp brow and looked up from the pot that was simmering on the black iron stove. "You're just in time for dinner, girls," she said. "Wash up quickly and set the table, please. The boys will be here in no time."

"Yes, ma'am," Caroline and Martha answered, heading for the washstand.

"Caroline was chosen for the spelling bee today, and she spelled every word perfectly, Mother," Martha said proudly. "She even spelled one that wasn't supposed to be hers!"

"Congratulations, Caroline," Mother praised.

"Your hard work certainly paid off," Grandma said.

Normally, Caroline would have been thrilled to tell Mother and Grandma how she had stood in front of the whole class and spelled all her words correctly. But all she could think about was Elsa's tear-stained face.

"What's keeping your brothers?" Mother said, lifting Thomas into his chair. "We must eat now or Caroline and Martha will be late getting back to school, so let us give thanks."

Caroline bowed her head and folded her hands as Mother and Grandma prayed aloud. The hot steam rising from the bowl of beans tickled her nose, and the mound of summer squash on her plate smelled delicious. But Caroline did not feel hungry at all.

"Eat up now, Caroline," Mother said before Caroline even noticed that everyone at the table was already eating, "or you'll never get to school in time for the rest of your lessons."

Picking up her fork, Caroline began pushing around squash and peas on her plate.

"Caroline!" Mother said. "Whatever is the

matter? Why aren't you eating?"

"She's still feeling sorry for Elsa, I'll bet," Martha interrupted, her mouth half full of bread. "I didn't feel sorry for her. Not in the least little bit. That girl's never said one nice word to anybody."

"Who is Elsa?" Mother asked.

"She's a girl in school who didn't know how to spell one of her words today. When Caroline got every letter right, Elsa was mad as a hornet," Martha said matter-of-factly. "She started crying and ran right out of the schoolhouse!"

"Goodness glory!" Mother exclaimed.

"I don't see why anyone should feel sorry for her," Martha continued. "She doesn't talk to anybody even when they're trying to be nice to her, and when she doesn't know how to spell a word, she makes up her very own letters!"

As Martha speared pieces of squash onto her fork, Mother turned her attention to Caroline. "Why do you think you feel so sorry for Elsa?"

"She talks funny, Mother. Maybe that's why she doesn't ever want to talk to anybody."

"What do you mean?" Mother asked.

"She says 'gay' instead of *g*," Caroline said. "And she shouts out silly things like 'Ah-bay-tsay . . .'"

"Why, she's speaking in German, Caroline." Mother smiled. "She's saying the alphabet, I think!"

"German?"

"German is another language, another way of speaking," Mother explained. "It's every bit as real a language as English. Years ago in Boston, a German family lived upstairs from my dressmaking shop. Listen carefully enough, Caroline, and you'll even hear some folks speaking it in town, especially those just settling in Brookfield. Elsa may not talk to you because she doesn't know how to speak English. You should be extra kind to her. Perhaps you can even help her learn faster."

Maybe Mother was right, and all Elsa needed was someone to teach her how to speak English. Maybe that explained why Elsa was so shy, and why Miss Morgan was so patient with her. Caroline didn't have any idea how to teach somebody English, but as she finally began to eat her squash and peas, she was determined to help somehow.

"Well, there you are!" Mother exclaimed as the door to the frame house flew open and Henry burst in.

Henry's curls were stuck to his sweaty forehead. "Sorry Mother, Joseph's hurt."

Leaning heavily on his brother's shoulder, Joseph hopped slowly into the room on one bare foot. His hair was caked with dirt, and his cotton shirt was stained. Looking closely at her oldest brother's face, Caroline was shocked to see that he was holding back tears.

"It hurts considerable, but it's not broken, I don't think." Joseph gritted his teeth and spoke as if every word pained him.

Once he was seated with his leg up, Mother knelt down and gently pressed her fingertips around Joseph's foot and ankle. "How in the world . . . ?" she began.

"There was a hole dug deep in the ground out where we were picking beans." Joseph frowned. "I never saw it there before."

"You'll not be walking on this ankle anytime

soon, I'm afraid." Mother looked up at Joseph. "It's already swollen, and I fear it'll get worse yet. Martha, as soon as you finish eating, I want you to go to town and find Dr. Hatch. We must be certain that Joseph hasn't broken a bone. I'm sorry, Caroline, but you'll have to return to the schoolhouse by yourself this afternoon."

"I could stay home, too, Mother, and help with Joseph's chores," Caroline offered. She was certain that she wouldn't be able to pay attention to her lessons when she was so concerned about her brother.

"No sense in both you and Martha missing your afternoon lessons," Mother said. "Tell Miss Morgan why Martha is staying at home."

Martha grinned at Caroline and Caroline scrunched up her nose in response as they both finished dinner.

Caroline decided to take the shortcut through the meadow back to school. Martha never wanted to go that way because she was afraid of getting her dress wet where they had to cross the creek. But Caroline didn't want to be late.

When she finally reached the creek's narrowest

point, she lifted the hem of her dress and climbed onto the three-boulder path that cut across the brook. Spreading her arms as far apart as possible, Caroline steadied herself on a smooth, flat rock and dipped her toes into the cool, bubbling water. A miniature rainbow mist hovered above the water droplets splashing off the sides of the boulders. Caroline bent down slowly and tried to touch the rainbow, but she couldn't reach it. At that very moment she heard a girl's voice above the gurgling water.

Caroline straightened up slowly and searched the creek bed for the sound. There, seated beneath a cluster of cattails, was Elsa, busily twisting stems into long yellow braids.

Elsa saw Caroline at the very same moment. Her happy, peaceful face filled with fear, and she quickly gathered up her pile of cattail braids, scrambled to her feet, and turned to flee.

"Wait!" Caroline hollered. "Please, Elsa! Wait!"

Elsa began to run, but Caroline scurried over the boulders and dashed after her. Within moments she caught Elsa by the sleeve.

"I know you were right at the spelling bee

today," Caroline began. "My mother told me you were speaking German. I didn't know you couldn't speak English."

Pushing her thick bangs out of her eyes, Elsa stared at Caroline, her gaze unwavering. "Elsa right," she finally said. "Elsa. No. Go. Back."

"But you must go back!" Caroline exclaimed. "You can sit next to me and Anna, and we'll try to help you learn words as best we can! Please, Elsa!"

Caroline reached out a hand toward Elsa. Elsa stared at her for many moments before she switched her cattail braids from one hand to the other and took Caroline's hand with a tiny smile. Together they left the marsh and headed toward the schoolhouse.

Caroline thought about what Mother had said during dinner, and she got a great idea. "Sun," she said, squinting up at the sky.

At first Elsa looked confused, but after a minute, she smiled and said, "*Sonne*. Sun."

"Tree," Caroline said, pointing at a maple in their path.

"*Baum,*" Elsa answered. "Terr-ee."

"Grass," Caroline said, kneeling and running her hands over a thick patch of dry grass.

"Gras," Elsa repeated. "Gr-a-ss."

"Right!" Caroline exclaimed proudly and pulled a black-eyed Susan out of the ground to show Elsa. "Flower," she said slowly, waiting for Elsa's response.

"Blume!" Elsa laughed back. "F . . . flowerr!"

By the time Caroline and Elsa ran up the schoolhouse steps, Elsa had learned a dozen new words, and Caroline had discovered a new friend.

WOLF

For almost a week, Joseph hobbled around on his sprained ankle, telling his younger brother and sisters how to do his chores. The day he was finally back on his feet, he found Caroline feeding chickens and said, "If you hurry up and finish with the chickens, you can go with Henry. He could use your help."

Caroline scooped up two dusty handfuls of grain and poured them into the bucket. "Help with what?" she asked curiously.

"Filling all the baskets you can carry with every wild, juicy berry that he doesn't eat first!"

"Really?" Caroline cried.

Caroline flew through her chores in no time and met Henry at the woodpile, two empty baskets swinging on each arm.

"We'll be back before dinner," Henry called out to Joseph. "Let's get a move on, little Brownbraid," he added with a wink. "I've been thinking about those berries all morning!"

The meadow behind the Quiners' barn was green and soft. Lacy, long-stemmed flowers brushed Caroline's skirt at every step. She longed to stop and pick a small bouquet, but she was already struggling to keep up with Henry's long strides.

"We can start picking any time now," Henry said, "though there are more and more berries the farther along we go."

Twirling around, Caroline wasn't certain where to begin. Wild raspberry and elderberry bushes grew all along the edge of the meadow, their tangled branches heavy with ripe, dark berries. Chokecherries swung from small trees and littered the ground. Closer to the earth, blueberry bushes brimmed with clusters of ripening berries. Caroline could not imagine

how there could possibly be more berries farther along. Already there were more berries
right in front of her than she had ever seen.

"Which ones should we pick?" Caroline
asked.

"Most anything you see," Henry answered,
and began pulling clusters of blueberries from
their bushes. "Mother will use every berry we
bring her, I bet. We don't have much time
before we have to head back for dinner, so I say
we race. First one to fill their baskets wins!"

In a flash, Henry was off to another blueberry patch. Caroline turned to the first wild
raspberry bush she saw. The sweet pink juice
stained her fingers as she tugged the berries
from the bush and dropped them gently in her
basket. Caroline tried as hard as she could to
think of picking berries instead of eating them.
But once half her basket was filled with the
wild raspberries, she couldn't resist any longer.
Race or no race, the next three picks ended up
in her mouth.

Caroline closed her eyes and savored the
sweet fruit. When she opened her eyes, she

found a furry gray-and-black face, a pointed muzzle, and two dark brown eyes looking up at her from a few feet away. Her throat tightened and her heart began to pound. Caroline knew it was a wolf.

"Don't move."

Caroline heard Henry's voice clearly, but he was too far back to step in before the wolf attacked. Biting her lip to keep it from shaking, she stared at the wolf's long face. He waved his bushy tail and watched her.

"Easy, boy." Henry's voice was closer now, but Caroline was terrifed. Clenching her fists, she closed her eyes so tightly, it hurt.

"Easy, boy." Henry's voice was right behind her now, but Caroline still couldn't move. It wasn't until she felt a sticky tongue on her fingers that she finally opened her eyes. Standing right beside her, his tail wagging, the wolf was licking her fingers.

"I reckon you didn't need me after all," Henry said as he knelt on the ground beside Caroline. "Good boy. That's a good old boy," he told the wolf. Gently Henry reached out and rubbed the back of his hand up and down the animal's long gray nose. "Where did you come from, huh? Who do you belong to?" he asked.

"I never heard of a wolf belonging to any-body!" Caroline said.

"So that's why you were so frightened," Henry cried out, laughing. "Silly Caroline! This isn't a wolf! He's a dog, is all."

"He looks just like a wolf, Henry!" she said defensively.

"He does," Henry admitted, "and if he fol-lows us home and Mother lets us keep him, I think we ought to call him Wolf."

The thought made Caroline sad. Their dog, Bones, had disappeared almost two years ago on the same day Father had set sail on a schooner. The schooner had capsized in a terri-ble storm, and neither Father nor Bones had ever returned home.

"Fill your baskets as high as you can, little Brownbraid," Henry said, breaking her thoughts, "so Mother might be pleased enough to let us keep him."

Caroline filled her baskets so high that a

plump, juicy berry or two tumbled out of each basket with almost every step she took on the way home. Wolf remained close by, walking along and gobbling up every stray berry that fell to the ground. As Caroline and Henry neared the little frame house, Wolf was still at Caroline's side.

Forgetting her fear, Caroline knelt down in front of Wolf. "I hope you'll be able to stay!" she whispered and hugged him so tight she could feel his cold, wet nose against her cheek. Wolf's soft brown eyes followed her every move, and he scrambled after her as she lifted her baskets and headed home with Henry.

Caroline and Henry led Wolf to the barn before bringing their pails of berries into the house.

"Have you ever seen berries so fine!" Mother exclaimed, giving Caroline a kiss. "They'll make a lovely dessert after dinner. Now let's sit down before it gets cold."

Caroline watched Henry pick at his food until he put down his fork and said, "Mother, what if someone found a dog that didn't belong to anybody partic'lar . . . ? It would be all right for it to become that person's new dog, wouldn't it?"

Mother put down her fork. "Have you found a dog?"

"Yes, ma'am," Henry admitted guiltily.

"Where did you find him?"

"Down by the creek. Caroline thought he was a wolf," Henry explained. "Scared her but good."

"How do you know he doesn't already have a family?" Mother asked.

"He found Caroline picking her berries, and he followed us all the way home, never once looking back. He's real pretty, Mother. He's gray and black, and very strong and—"

"You know full well that we didn't get another dog after Bones disappeared because we couldn't feed one, Henry. It's hard enough keeping food on the table for all the children in this family. No sense in taking on another mouth to feed." Mother's tone now clearly told Caroline that the discussion was over. With a sigh of disappointment, Caroline looked over at her brother.

"What if the dog didn't eat much?" Henry persisted. "What if I made sure he only ate left-over table scraps or berries or other such things I could find for him?"

"We don't have leftover table scraps, Henry-O," Mother said. "And it makes no sense to keep an animal that we cannot keep fed and healthy. It isn't fair to the poor dog."

"Yes, ma'am," Henry answered, staring intently at his plate. A minute later, he looked up grinning. "Woodchucks!" he cried out.

"Excuse me, Henry?" Mother said.

"The woodchucks in the garden. The ones terrorizing the squash and the peas. Didn't you just tell me last week that you wished there was some way to get rid of them once and for all?"

"Well, yes, but—" Mother began.

"Well, don't dogs love to chase woodchucks? Wolf would be a perfect watchdog, and your garden would be safe again!" Henry grinned.

The whole family couldn't help but smile at Henry's reasoning. Even Mother shook her head and laughed.

"Oh, Henry-O, sometimes you remind me

so much of your father. Very well, your Wolf may stay. But keep him in the barn, and no table scraps. You'll have to make sure he gets enough to eat elsewhere."

Caroline and Henry grinned at each other across the table. "Yes, ma'am!" they cried out together.

THE INDIAN

True to Henry's word, the woodchucks quickly scurried off to dig new burrows far away from Wolf. It was autumn, and the garden was bursting with cucumbers, peas, lima beans, corn, sweet potatoes, squash, onions, turnips, and potatoes.

One morning, Mother announced that Thomas and the girls would accompany her to the general store to buy pickling supplies to preserve all their fresh vegetables for the winter. She looked over the children one by one, until she was satisfied that they were neat and clean enough for the trip into town.

The sun rose slowly through rolling clouds. The meadows were awash in amber and lavender as goldenrod and asters bid the summer farewell. Father had loved autumn more than any other season, and Caroline always missed him most at this time of year.

When they finally arrived at the crossroads of town, Mother led the children across deep ruts in the dirt road, weaving in and out of the small circles of chattering townsfolk. Mr. Carpenter waved and called out to them.

"Hello, Benjamin," Mother said. "Are you running errands, too?"

Mr. Carpenter looked serious. "I'm afraid Sarah's taken a fever. I've just picked up this medicine from the doctor," he said, pulling out a vial of liquid from his pocket.

"That's a shame," Mother said. "I shall bring over a crock of soup for her."

"That's kind of you," he said, waving good-bye. "I'll give Sarah your best."

But before they could say good-bye to Mr. Carpenter, a deep, furious voice burst forth from behind Caroline. "You! You!" At the foot of the stoop, an Indian stood glaring at a table of men playing checkers. His head was shaved clean except for a narrow stripe of bristly black hair that cut across his gleaming scalp. Bold scarlet and white streaks were painted across his cheeks, arms, and bare chest, and Caroline could see the rage in the man's piercing black eyes.

Mother pulled Thomas into her arms. "Martha, take Eliza! Caroline, give me your hand. We must go! And no commotion, any of you!"

"You! Kill! Murder brother of Black Horse!" the Indian said. Whipping a thin silver knife out of his boot, he held the flashing blade up against one of the checker player's necks.

"I didn't do it! I didn't kill anybody," the man said.

Trying her best to be quiet, Caroline took Mother's hand. Then she heard Mr. Carpenter's clear, firm voice say, "There must be some misunderstanding here. Carleton can't even beat a man at checkers. How could he take someone's life?"

Mother's firm hand quickly guided Caroline

and the rest of the children off the stoop and down onto the side of the road. Caroline looked back and saw Mr. Carpenter gesturing to the Indian. Much to her surprise, the painted man jumped onto a sleek black mare and galloped off down the road. Soon Caroline could no longer see the man or his horse on the horizon. He had disappeared as quickly as he had appeared.

"The good Lord spare you, Benjamin! Taking such a risk!" Mother said when Mr. Carpenter caught up with them.

"No risk there, Charlotte." Mr. Carpenter shrugged. "One lone man can't stand up against a whole pack of townsfolk, no matter how crazed with anger he is. Truth be told, I was more worried for the Indian than for Carleton."

"Did he hurt Mr. Carleton?" Caroline asked. Her heart was still pounding, and she had never before felt so frightened and confused. Father had had many friends who were Indians, and though she often didn't understand what they said, they had always been kind to her.

"No, little Brownbraid," Mr. Carpenter said soothingly. "Carleton's fine."

"Mr. Ben saved his life! Right in front of our eyes!" Martha exclaimed, her eyes shining with admiration.

"Didn't do anything of the sort!" Mr. Carpenter's laugh rang loud. "That poor Indian didn't understand one word I was saying. Come on up here, young Thomas," he said, and swung the toddler up on his shoulders. "How 'bout a song to walk to?"

> *"Old Dan Tucker was a fine old man,*
> *He washed his face in the frying pan,*
> *He combed his hair with a wagon wheel*
> *And died of the toothache in his heel.*
> *Git out the way for Old Dan Tucker!*
> *He's too late to git his supper.*
> *Supper's over and dishes washed,*
> *Nothing left but a piece of squash!"*

Caroline laughed out loud as Mr. Carpenter sang the silly words. But a part of her couldn't stop thinking about the Indian with the painted face who called himself Black Horse, coming to town, bringing noise and fights. If he ever came to town again, Caroline hoped she'd be far out of his way.

Peacock Feathers

Mother, Grandma, and the girls spent long days and evenings pickling and preserving. Each morning, once Mother and Grandma finished slicing the vegetables, Caroline and Martha packed the juicy chunks into wooden barrels. When each barrel was piled high, Mother poured in a mixture of vinegar, water, salt, and spices. The sharp brine stung Caroline's nose and lingered in the frame house.

"Charlie's just come by with word that his mother's fever's broke for good," Joseph burst into the house and told Mother. "He says she wanted you to be the first to know that she's finally on the mend."

"Thank heavens," Mother said with relief. "The poor thing suffered bouts of fever for over two weeks!" Stirring the simmering fruit with vigorous strokes, she added, "Living as we are, surrounded by all these swamps and lowlands, it's a wonder we all haven't caught the chill fever. Had Father and I known what the swamps would bring us, we surely would never have settled so close to them.

"Joseph, is Henry watching Thomas and Eliza?" Mother suddenly asked.

"They're out playing by the woodpile," Joseph replied quickly. "Henry's working right next to them, practically."

"Send them inside before you leave, please, Joseph," Mother directed. "And be careful in those woods."

"Yes, ma'am." Joseph nodded, closing the door behind him.

Caroline looked questioningly at Martha. "Do you s'pose she's still worried on account of Old Dan Tucker?" she whispered.

"Who?" Martha whispered back.

"Old Dan Tucker. The Indian with the painted face!"

"Let's not even talk about *him*!" Martha shuddered. "It's too scary to think about."

Caroline thought back to the moment they had arrived at the frame house after their visit to the general store. Mother had pulled Joseph aside, and Caroline could tell by Joseph's grave manner at dinner that Mother had told him about the trouble in town. After supper that night, while the girls embroidered their samplers and Grandma knitted, Joseph took the rifle down from its hook above the door and set it on the table. Under Mother's watchful eye, he carefully cleaned and loaded it.

Now the girls went back to pickling, and the house was quiet. Caroline was gathering the last of the cucumbers when the door crashed open against the washstand.

As Caroline whirled around, Martha shrieked and flung her hands up to her mouth. The Indian with the painted face was in the kitchen.

"Be quiet, girls," Mother commanded. She moved next to Caroline and motioned Martha to her side. Even if Caroline had wanted to move, she was stiff with fear.

"What is it you want?" Mother finally asked. Caroline could not believe how calmly she spoke.

The house remained silent until Caroline heard the soft padding of moccasined feet crossing the wooden floorboards. The Indian was headed into the parlor, where Grandma was napping in the daybed.

Caroline was terrified as she watched from the doorway, but it was a flowered glass vase that interested the Indian, not Grandma. He pulled a handful of peacock feathers out of the vase and pushed them into his long, braided hair. The scarlet stripes of war paint hid his features, and though his black eyes were no longer flashing with anger, the peacock feathers poking out of his braid gave him a wild and exotic look.

He picked up a thimble, a spool of thread, and Grandma's crochet needles. Then he reached for Caroline's sampler, and she held her breath as he turned it every which way before finally setting it back on the table. He clasped his hand around the thimble and spool of thread just as Henry came barreling into the house with Joseph close on his heels.

"We found Hog!" Henry cried. "Let's eat!"

"We have a guest," Mother said as the Indian turned and stared at Joseph and Henry.

Caroline watched the color drain out of her brothers' faces. Joseph glanced at the rifle on the table, but his eyes met Mother's and he silently stood his ground.

"Man!" the Indian said unexpectedly.

"What man?" Mother asked.

"Man of house!" he answered.

"There is no man here," Mother answered. "Only my boys."

The Indian walked over to Henry and Joseph and stood in front of them, arms folded across his chest. He nodded his head and pointed at Henry. "Brother?" he asked, staring at Joseph.

"Yes," Joseph answered.

Turning back to the table, the Indian picked up a crock of preserves and left the house without another word, the peacock feathers in his hair fluttering with each step.

The entire house let out a great sigh and Caroline tried hard not to cry with relief. Then Mother dashed outside to gather Thomas and Eliza, who had missed the whole episode, playing out on the other side of the house. As Mother hugged them all tightly, Henry asked, "Do you think that Indian will ever come back?"

"I don't believe so," Mother answered. "He's still looking for the man who killed his brother. He knows he won't find what he's looking for in this house."

GRANDMA SAYS GOOD-BYE

After the weather turned colder, Grandma received a letter from Father's younger brother. Uncle Elisha's wife had suddenly taken ill. Uncle Elisha asked that Grandma come to Milwaukee and help care for his sons while he nursed his wife back to health. As Caroline listened with a lump in her throat, Mother insisted that Grandma go to Milwaukee. She was smiling at Grandma, but her eyes were full of sadness. "Elisha needs you now, and you must go to him. The children and I will manage fine, though we'll miss you terribly."

Caroline wanted to protest, but she didn't

dare. She knew Mother would chide her, so she thought about Uncle Elisha instead. She didn't care for Father's brother, even though she had no reason to dislike him. It had been two years since she had seen her uncle. One gray afternoon, he had arrived at their little frame house with Grandma and his sister, Aunt Margaret, bringing news that Father's schooner had been lost at sea. Caroline hated to think about that terrible day.

Now, another sad day was coming. Uncle Elisha would arrive from Milwaukee once again, and Grandma would go to live with him and Caroline's cousins William, George Henry, and John. Caroline couldn't help wishing that Uncle Elisha would never visit again. Every time he came and went, she was left with an aching loneliness that took too long to go away.

Footsteps thumped up the stairs and Caroline turned to find Martha's dark eyes peering at her through the stair railing. "Mother says come down now," Martha said. "She says we must spend all the time we can with Grandma, seeing how she's leaving tomorrow."

Caroline looked back at the oak tree and the crooked, black limbs shuddering in the wind.

"What are you doing?" Martha asked. Climbing the last two steps, she passed the beds and the curtain that divided the room to look out the window. "What are you looking at, anyway?"

"Nothing," Caroline replied glumly.

"Then come downstairs," Martha said. "Don't you want to be with Grandma before she goes away? If I were you, I'd rather be downstairs with Grandma than up here all by myself." With a whirl of her brown woolen skirt, Martha was off, braids and bows flouncing about as she went down the stairs.

Mother appeared a few moments later. "What's keeping you, Caroline?" she asked. "I expect you to come downstairs this minute."

Head bowed, Caroline sighed. "Yes, ma'am." Then she took a deep breath, shivering again as she crossed the cold, drafty floorboards to the stairs.

"Whatever is wrong?" Mother asked, lifting Caroline's chin.

Caroline tried not to cry in front of Mother, but she just couldn't help it. Tears spilled down her cheeks as she began, "I wish, I wish . . ."

Mother pulled Caroline close against her. Her black woolen dress was rough and scratchy, but Caroline didn't mind. She wished she could hold on to Mother forever.

"I wish Grandma could stay with us, too, but Uncle Elisha needs her now," Mother whispered in her ear. "Milwaukee isn't so far away. We'll see Grandma again next year. Now we must get downstairs. Grandma is waiting for you."

Caroline followed Mother down the stairs. Grandma was rocking slowly in front of the hearth, Henry, Martha, and Eliza seated at her feet. Thomas bounced lightly on her knee, and Joseph leaned against the far side of the hearth. Grandma was telling one of her stories, and the whole room was still, listening.

"There you are, my dear," Grandma greeted Caroline. "Come and sit."

Henry moved over and Caroline sat down beside him, smoothing her dress over her crossed legs. "You didn't miss anything yet,"

Henry informed her. "Father's five years old in this story, and he's decided he wants to shoot his first deer."

Grandma smiled and began again. "Day and night your father talked about getting his first buck, and begged his papa to take him along on the first hunt of the winter. That morning Henry was up 'fore anybody, so full of excitement you'd think he'd about burst. I sent him on his way with your grandfather, expecting to see them back 'fore supper. Well, early in the afternoon, just after dinner, Henry slipped in through the door, his cheeks two red dots, his hair all mussed up, his boots full of snow and ice."

"What happened to him, Grandma?" Martha straightened up on her knees and asked.

"I asked exactly that, Martha, and he said, 'Papa went off scouting and told me to be real quiet while I was waiting for him. He said deer could be walking by 'most anytime. Sure enough a whole herd came through the trees, and I didn't have anything to shoot 'em with, and I couldn't yell for Papa,'" Grandma continued in a voice that sounded like five-year-old Father's. "'So I started real slow, backing away and thinking I could get out of sight and find Papa without scaring off the deer. I walked two or three steps, Mama,' he said, 'then all of a sudden I couldn't move. I was stuck to something and I couldn't go anywhere.'"

"What'd he get stuck to?" Henry jumped in as Grandma paused to take a breath.

"A corner of his scarf had come undone and fastened itself to a tree branch behind him." Grandma smiled, her skin crinkling all around her bright eyes. "He pulled and tugged at that scarf, but it wouldn't come loose. I had tucked it around him so tight, he was stuck but good. Your father stood fastened to that tree for a long time, still he never hollered or made a fuss because he didn't want to scare off the deer."

"Did Grandpa find him?" Joseph asked. He was standing straight up now, his arms folded across his chest.

"No, the deer found him first," Grandma replied. "Seems a yearling had happened upon the scene and was quietly watching him. The deer was soon joined by others, and Henry got so spooked that he finally tore through the yarn on one side of his scarf, wriggled out of it, and ran off through the woods fast as he could.

"An hour or so later, he found Grandpa with his gun cocked and ready to shoot. Lord save me if that deer didn't have part of Henry's scarf stuck in his antlers!"

"How did the scrap of scarf get on the deer's antler?" Joseph asked.

"Your father never could figure!" Grandma chuckled. "But suddenly he couldn't bear to see the young thing killed. He decided to scream and holler, and make enough noise to send all the living things in the forest scurrying away lickety-split!"

"Goodness glory!" Mother exclaimed. "Henry never told me this story, Mother Quiner. What did Father Quiner do when Henry was making all that noise?"

"Near jumped right out of his skin, to hear Henry tell it," Grandma answered. "Your grandfather was so stunned by all the hollering, he jerked his rifle up and shot at all the leaves and branches and sky above. Served William right, I declared, taking such a little one off hunting like he was a grown-up."

"Did Father get a caning?" Henry asked.

"He ran off before your grandfather could catch him. By the time your grandfather arrived with news that young Henry had disappeared, he was so relieved to see his boy in front of the hearth, he didn't think twice about missing that deer."

By then, the sun had long since slipped into the night sky and it was time to say good night. Uncle Elisha would arrive way past the children's bed time to take Grandma back with him. Caroline cried when she hugged her good-bye, and as she finally fell off to sleep, Caroline wished away the winter. Next year had to come soon, so she could be with Grandma again.

CHRISTMAS TRUNK

The week after Caroline's eighth birthday, and a week before Christmas, Mother announced that she'd received a letter from Uncle Elisha. "Grandma has settled in just fine," Mother said as she swiftly chopped turnips and potatoes for a stew. "He said that his wife's health is slowly improving, and that he is very busy at the newspaper keeping up on stories about the war with Mexico."

"Does Uncle Elisha say how much longer we'll be at war, Mother?" Joseph asked.

"I don't believe so," Mother said.

"I wish I could go off to war," Joseph said.

"Well, I am happy you cannot," Mother replied. "We need you right here at the moment—"

A loud *thump, thump, THUMP!* interrupted Mother, and all heads turned toward the door. "Who on earth could possibly be traveling through all this snow?" Mother asked.

With a vigorous tug, she pulled the door open, and a gust of winter air and a whirling cloud of snow blew into the house. There was a tall, stocky man and a young girl whose tightly wrapped scarf hid everything but a pair of sparkling blue eyes and a brown curl.

"Anna!" Caroline sprang up and ran to the door to hug her friend.

"Forgive us, ma'am," Mr. Short said quickly, "to come in like this, no word or warning 't all." Running his hand over his brown curls, he wiped away the melting snowflakes that were beginning to trickle down his brow. "Today Anna and me, we went to the general store," he explained. "The mail came and Anna heard a man say he had a trunk to deliver. A trunk for a family Quiner. Anna near leaped out of her boots, begging me to carry the trunk to the wagon and bring it to your family."

"Where could such a trunk have come from?" Mother wondered.

Mr. Short shrugged. "I will carry it in and you will see, right?"

Anna's eyes twinkled with excitement. "I thought that if I had such a trunk waiting for me, I wouldn't want it sitting all alone in some store. I'd want to open it soon as I could. So I asked Papa to bring it here. I hope you don't mind, Mrs. Quiner."

"Mind? Why, of course not, Anna!" Mother hugged her. "You've done a very kind thing for all of us. If it hadn't been for you, that trunk would have been at the general store for days."

"Maybe Uncle Elisha and Grandma sent it!" Martha cried.

"Maybe it's from some stranger we never saw before," Henry suggested. "Maybe it's a trunkful of Christmas surprises!"

"Maybe it came from Boston," Joseph said. "Maybe Grandma and Grandpa Tucker sent it."

"I'm afraid we'll just have to wait and see," Mother said.

By then, Mr. Short had stepped out of the blowing snow and Joseph helped him carry the trunk inside. He grasped one side of the trunk, and step by step they slid it across the floorboards, leaving a sloppy trail of snow and ice from the door to the hearth.

"Will you be staying for supper?" Mother asked as she mopped up the wet floor.

"Thank you, but no, ma'am," Mr. Short said. "Come, Anna. We must go now."

"But Papa! Can't we stay to see what's inside? Oh, please, Papa!"

"Anna, you and your father have come so far out of your way already," Mother said gently. "And your mother will surely be keeping supper. If your father says you must go now, you must go."

"The child's mother is no longer living, ma'am," Mr. Short interrupted brusquely. "Anna and me lost her three years back."

Caroline had always wondered why Anna's mother was never with Anna and her father.

Her throat suddenly tight, and her eyes beginning to burn, she turned to her friend. Impulsively, she grabbed Anna's hand and gave it a warm squeeze.

Mother caught her breath. "Oh, I am so sorry!" she said, smiling kindly at Anna and Mr. Short. "Surely then, you and Anna must stay and sup with us this evening."

"Don't want to be no trouble, ma'am," Mr. Short said quickly.

"No trouble at all," Mother assured him. "We'd love to have your company, but I must warn you, we're fresh out of coffee. I'll oven-roast some barley and make it into a toddy that will warm us just fine."

"We don't have to wait until after supper to find out what's in this trunk, do we, Mother?" Henry asked woefully.

"Of course not, Henry." Mother laughed. "For once, I can't wait any longer than you!"

By the time Mother had finished wiping all the snow and ice off the heavy wooden trunk, everyone in the room was clustered around her, waiting impatiently to see what treasure it held. Expertly jamming an iron poker beneath the rim, Mr. Short opened the trunk without scraping or cracking the wood.

Fingers shaking with excitement, Mother reached in and picked up the note placed on the small stack of magazines at the top of the trunk. "It *is* from Boston," she said as she unfolded the letter. "'Greetings to you, dear Charlotte, and the children,'" she read aloud. "'And gifts to all of you from all of us. May the Lord bless you this Christmas. Mama.'

"Here's a *Godey's Lady's Book,* and two copies of *Saturday Evening Post,*" she said, "a copy of *Home Journal* and *The Christian World.* I've never seen either of these before. Look, children! Here are three copies of *Youth's Companion.* Grandma's sent you your very own magazines, too!" Pausing for a moment, Mother turned to look at the children, her eyes full of mischief. "Shall we stop here and wait until after supper to see what's underneath?"

"No!" six young voices shouted merrily.

"No, no, no!" Thomas mimicked.

Beneath the magazines, Mother discovered

three books: *The Deerslayer*, by James Fenimore Cooper; *A Christmas Carol*, by Charles Dickens; and a small book of stories by Hans Christian Andersen. Beneath the books, she found an assortment of small cans.

"I do believe there is food in these cans!" she exclaimed.

Caroline had never before heard of food that came out of a can, and she watched closely, her eyes growing rounder and rounder as Mother lifted each item from the trunk. "Here are some Boston baked beans, and a can of cranberries. Goodness glory! They've even sent a can with Boston brown bread inside!" Mother turned the can over and over, studying it from top to bottom. "Is it possible someone's baked the bread in the can and sealed it?" she asked in awe.

Then Mother pulled small packages of olives and capers and dried codfish from the trunk, along with jars of currant jelly, pickled cauliflower, ginger, and macaroni, and a small box of tea. "We won't have to worry about oven-roasting the barley now." She laughed, showing the tea leaves to Anna's father.

"It's like someone sent us a whole general store in a trunk!" Caroline exclaimed as Mother again reached into the wide wooden box.

"Why, I never!" Mother exclaimed. Pulling out a bolt of red gingham, a bolt of wool dyed a rich navy blue, and a bolt of gold silk brocade, she ran her fingertips softly over the brand-new material. "I'm certain there's enough here for all of us, if I use them well," Mother said, and Caroline could tell by the thoughtful look in Mother's eyes that she was already planning the dresses and shirts and trousers she'd soon be cutting out and sewing.

"I shall put them away somewhere safe, and wait for an extra-special occasion."

At the bottom of the trunk, Mother found a special gift for the boys: a small checkerboard accompanied by two packs of checkers.

"Let's play, Joseph!" Henry cried.

"You may play after supper," Mother said firmly. Reaching far down into the trunk, she pulled out the last items, three pairs of girls' shoes, each a different size. The shoes had been worn, but were made of fine brown leather that wasn't scratched or stained or worn through. Caroline stared at those shoes and hoped with all her might that one pair would fit her just right.

"You're so lucky," Anna said breathlessly. Caroline only nodded her response.

Soon after supper, as the frosty white glow of daylight disappeared outside the window-panes and night fell, Caroline hugged Anna and said good-bye. Handing a can of Boston baked beans to Mr. Short, Mother thanked him again.

After Mother shut the door, she sat in the rocker and reached for one of the books she had pulled from the trunk earlier that afternoon.

Joseph and Henry quietly jumped each other's checkers. Martha sat at Mother's feet, a dozing Thomas curled up on her lap. Caroline took Eliza's hand and together they sat on the other side of Mother's rocker, beside the blazing heat from the fire.

"'The Little Mermaid, by Hans Christian Andersen,'" Mother began.

"'Far out in the ocean, the water is as blue as the petals of the loveliest cornflower, and as clear as the purest glass.'"

"What's a ocean?" Eliza interrupted.

"Miles and miles of blue water and waves as far as your eye can see, Eliza. An ocean is even bigger than a lake or a river," Mother replied.

"Is there an ocean in Boston, Mother?" Martha asked.

"Yes, Martha," Mother answered. "The Atlantic Ocean."

"I wish I could see the ocean," Martha said wistfully.

Leaning against her sister, Caroline wished with all her heart she could see the place called Boston, where Mother had lived, the place where all the wonderful treasures in the Christmas trunk had journeyed from. But not now. At this very moment, with the fire warming her back, and the wind shrieking outside the snow-covered windowpanes, Caroline couldn't imagine any place she'd rather be than snug inside her house.

January Thaw

After the excitement of Christmas and her birthday, Caroline always grew tired of winter. She was bored with the long months of snow and wind and longed for the far-off summer days when she could run outside with her sisters and brothers, free of heavy scarves and woollen socks.

But one morning in January, Caroline woke to find that the sky was a bold, endless blue and the brown fields were dotted with gray mounds of snow that seemed to shrink right before Caroline's eyes.

"It's spring!" Caroline breathed. "Winter's

gone! Spring is here!"

"Shush, silly!" Martha grumbled from the far side of the bed. "Spring doesn't come in January!"

"It seems we're having a January thaw, girls." Mother smiled at them through the railing. "Wake the others, now. Let's not waste a moment of this glorious day!"

After they raced through their chores, Mother told the girls that their studies could wait. Caroline couldn't believe it. They were free to spend the day outside in the sun.

"But you must wear your shoes, girls, and your shawls, too," Mother cautioned. "It may feel like a warm spring day, but there's still a chill in the air, and the ground will be cold and wet."

A cool breeze greeted Caroline as she stepped out of the frame house, ruffling her shawl and the green ribbon that was tied in a bright bow at the bottom of her braid. Caroline breathed in the refreshing air and grinned happily as warm sunlight spilled onto her face.

"How 'bout a game of poison tag?" Henry

shouted to his sisters as they raced to the woodpile.

Caroline looked down at her shoes that had arrived in the Christmas trunk. They looked and felt newer than any shoes she had ever worn, and they were much, much finer than Martha's hand-me-down shoes. Fashioned out of soft brown leather, the new shoes had laces that climbed all the way up Caroline's ankle. The melting snow had left a muddy slush in the yard, and Caroline couldn't bear the thought of thick mud coating her new shoes. She looked at both her brothers running barefoot.

You must wear your shoes, girls. But even as Mother's words rang in her ears, Caroline made her decision. She carefully unlaced her shoes and peeled off her scratchy wool stockings. Shivers shot up and down her legs and spine as puddles of icy-cold water sprang up around her feet, but she felt so free. "Well, if you don't have to wear any shoes, then I'm not going to, either!" Martha huffed, untying her own laces as quickly as she could.

Then Henry tagged Caroline and cried out,

"You're it, little Brownbraid," and the game of poison tag began. Caroline chased after her siblings until her feet no longer stung from the cold and she was out of breath with laughter.

When poison tag was over, Martha said to Caroline and Eliza, "Let's go down by the creek. The grass is so wet, it'll make perfect dolls!"

"Yes! Come on, Wolf," Caroline called as she helped little Eliza take off her own shoes, too. The three girls raised their skirt hems above their ankles and ran past the garden and barn. It was the most fun Caroline could ever remember having in January.

"Wait here, Eliza—we'll get the grass," Martha said when they got to the mucky, ice-cold marsh beside the creek.

"It's just the right length for dolls!" Caroline exclaimed. Lifting her skirt to her knees, she waded in after Martha.

Eliza waited impatiently with Wolf as her sisters yanked handfuls of tall grass from the marsh. When their arms were full, they dunked the grass into the icy water at their feet and pulled it out dripping wet. Holding up their skirts with one hand and the wet grass close against their shawls with the other, they trudged back to more solid ground, thick, heavy mud tugging at their ankles with every step.

They found a spot on the bank that looked dry and placed the grass they had collected in a pile. Pulling their shawls from their shoulders, they folded and laid them on the ground. "Sit, Wolf. And you, too, Eliza. Here, next to me," Caroline said. "I'll help you make your doll."

Caroline held a handful of grass tightly and ran her other hand across the shaft from end to end until all the blades of grass stuck together and all the edges were smooth. Then, looping the shaft over and lining up the ends, she said, "Hold this, Eliza, while I tie the neck."

Eliza held the grass loop still while Caroline tied a single thick blade of grass tightly around the top of the shaft, just below the loop. "There's the head!" Caroline said. Spreading out the grass from side to side in the little circle she'd just made, she quickly fashioned a perfectly round head. Then she fanned the two separate columns of grass below the head into one long trunk. "Now for the arms," she said, lifting up a few blades of grass from the left and right sides of the doll's body and tying them together at the tips with a single blade of grass. "And the waist," she continued, tying another blade of grass tightly about the middle of the doll, giving it a long grass skirt. "Perfect!" she exclaimed.

"Oh, Caroline"—Eliza clapped—"she's so pretty!"

Caroline had been so busy making the doll that she hadn't even noticed that her dress was soaked through where she was sitting on her icy, damp shawl. And now her feet and toes were tingling, and her petticoats were drenched and lying heavy and wet against her legs.

Caroline felt a lump growing in her throat. Dirt was smeared across her wet garments from poison tag, and clumps of wet brown grass hung from her dress and apron. Mother was not going to be happy.

Just then, Henry's voice reached up to the creek bed. "Girls, dinner time!" He was panting when he reached them. "Better hurry. Mother was spitting mad when she saw Joseph and me running with no shoes on." He looked at his sisters' soaked, muddy dresses.

Guiltily the girls ran back toward the house, feet smarting and teeth beginning to chatter.

Mother was waiting for them outside. "I've found the shoes and socks you are supposed to be wearing," Mother said sharply. "Where are your shawls?"

"Back by the creek where we were making grass dolls," Caroline stammered.

"You girls are a mess. Soaked through to the bone and numb with cold. You should know better. Leave your clothes by the hearth, and get upstairs under your quilt without another word. I'll go fetch your shawls."

Caroline followed her sisters upstairs. Mother was right. They'd been so foolish. Now the perfect day was ruined, and Caroline was a mess. Reaching behind her back, she gingerly pulled her long, brown braid over her shoulder. Her precious green bow was not at the bottom.

Caroline dropped her head into her hands. She could feel the tears welling up inside her.

"What's wrong with you?" Martha snapped.

"I . . . I . . . lost my bow," Caroline sobbed into her shaky hands.

"The green one that you got for your birthday?" Martha asked, her eyes wide.

Caroline nodded miserably.

"That's awful!" said her sister, who understood how losing such a beautiful thing could make someone cry. "It'll be all right. Look Caroline, we can make necklaces for our dolls while we're waiting for Mother to come back," Martha said, trying to cheer Caroline. "I saved all the berries and the twigs you found, and a couple long strings of grass, besides. Here," she said, opening her cupped hands and pouring half of her berry-and-pinecone mix into Caroline's hand.

By the time Mother finally came back with their shawls, Caroline's tears were dry and she'd changed into clean clothes.

When Mother called them down to dinner, she pulled Caroline aside. "I think you lost more than your shawl down by the creek, little Brownbraid," Mother said, and in her hand was the shiny green ribbon clean and good as new.

THE RESTING PLACE

The next week, the snow returned and their January thaw felt like a slip of a dream to Caroline. She was freezing as she and Mother ran their errands in town.

"Thank you for fixing the heel so quickly," Mother said to Mr. June, the shoemaker. "The shoes looked so new at Christmastime, I didn't imagine they'd lose a heel in the blink of an eye."

"Balderdash, Mrs. Quiner!" the shoemaker replied, pulling two heel pegs from between his thin lips and plunking them down on the bench beside him. "Didn't take but a peg or two, right here at the tip of the heel." He turned the shoe in his hands, carefully examining the sole. "Mmm," he finally said, smiling down at Caroline and revealing two rows of brown-and-gold teeth. "My guess is it was worn by a shuffler before you, child."

"A shuffler?" Caroline asked.

"No doubt about it." He nodded, rubbing his stubbly chin with his knuckles. "A pair of shoes with leather this new couldn't possibly have a heel fall off unless a shuffler's broke them in."

Perplexed, Caroline said, "I've never heard of a shuffler before, sir."

Mr. June bent his knees and slowly walked across the tiny shop, scuffling the soles and heels of his shoes over the floorboards: *chhh, chhh, chhh, chhh.* It looked like a funny dance to Caroline, and she tried not to giggle. " 'Pick up your feet! Save your shoes,' I always tell the shufflers. But they never listen!" he exclaimed, arms flailing. "Those heels have taken a beating, Mrs. Quiner, and truth be told, the soles could follow suit at any time."

"We'll surely keep an eye on them, won't we,

Caroline?" Mother prompted.

"Yes, ma'am," Caroline agreed. Tilting her foot up, she studied the bottom of the shoe she had just finished lacing up her ankle.

Mother tied and tucked Caroline's scarf around her head and neck while Caroline buttoned her coat. With a final thank-you and good-bye to the shoemaker, they stepped out of the shop. Joseph was just leaving the general store, and he hurried toward them, snow swirling frantically around him.

"Let's get back to the house now, before this storm gets any worse," Mother said. "I should never have had us venture out today, I fear. But the wind didn't seem half bad before dinner."

Icy snow whipped at Caroline's face, nipping her cheeks and stinging her eyes as she followed Mother and Joseph home. The prickly wool scarf that covered her nose and mouth grew damper with each frosty breath and began scratching the back of her neck. Plodding through crusty layers of snow, Caroline cringed as chunks of ice found their way into the space between her woolen socks and her leather shoes. A cold dampness seeped into her socks, and the wet wool began to chafe her ankles. Caroline ducked her head against the wind, and when Mother and Joseph stopped abruptly, Caroline bumped headfirst into the folds of Mother's long gray coat.

Just ahead, two figures were trudging down the road toward them. The taller figure held the reins of a thin, brown horse. A leather harness stretched tightly over the horse's shoulders, and as the figures moved closer, Caroline could see the narrow travois that the horse dragged behind it. Two long poles, trailing at an angle from the horse's back to the snowy ground, had strips of bark and straps of leather tautly woven around and between them to form a low bed. The foot of the travois rested just above the snow. Its poles left two thin trails following horseshoe prints as it bumped along the road.

The horse moved slowly past Caroline, and she stole a look at the travois. An old man with thick white hair lay there, covered in a blanket that was patched together with brown, gray, and black furs. His brown face was etched with deep wrinkles, and his black eyes stared blankly at the troubled sky.

"No-taw-kah!" A woman's voice rose above the wind. "Ask where we are to go!"

"I will find it, Mother," another voice answered. When Caroline looked up from behind Mother's skirt, she quickly realized the voice was from a tall boy not much older than Joseph.

"We near the end," the woman said. "We must ask." A fur robe was gathered close about her neck and shoulders, hiding all but her face and buckskin mittens. Her long, black hair, speckled with snowflakes, disappeared beneath the dense black robe. The woman's drawn face and tired eyes belied the strength of her voice.

"What is it you need?" Mother asked. "Perhaps we can help."

"We must find the place where boulders and firs stand watch by running water," she called out above the wind. "We have strayed from the path that has taken us there before. Do you know this place?"

"She could be talking about the creek that

runs through the back of our land," Joseph said.

"But the boulders don't sit and watch our creek, Joseph. They sit right *in* it," Caroline chimed in from behind Mother, glad to know something helpful during this strange moment in the snowstorm.

"You're right," Joseph agreed. "Maybe she means the creek outside town that passes by the mill."

Mother pointed at the travois. "Surely this man needs help. We have a doctor in this town. My son can take you to him."

"We have journeyed far," the woman said, her eyes full of sorrow. "We have brought my son's grandfather to rest with Manitou in the land of his birth. He has little breath left and needs no doctor. He lives only to see his resting place."

Mother nodded. "Perhaps someone else in town will know this place you speak about."

"I don't think we should take them into the tavern or the general store, Mother," Joseph said, quietly enough so the wind wouldn't carry his words to the people trailing behind. "When I walked into the store, I heard Mr. Porter and two other men complaining about the Indians who keep coming back and roaming through the countryside, helping themselves to folks' crops and running off with their livestock."

"These people have done no such thing, Joseph," Mother scolded. "They've come to bury the boy's grandfather, and were your father here this minute, he would be searching up and down every creek this side of Milwaukee until he found those boulders and fir trees. He would have seen to it that the old man looked on his birthplace one last time before he died. I intend to do no less!"

"But what about the Indian who came to our house? He took our peacock feathers and left with a crock of our preserves!" Caroline said.

"That man was trying to find the white man who killed his brother. Mr. Carpenter told us as much," Mother said. "Besides, he did us no harm."

"But he came into our house, Mother," Caroline said. "He took our things. . . ."

"There are good and bad men of all kinds, Caroline," Mother said sharply. "If it weren't for Father's Indian friends bringing us meat last winter, who knows where we might have found food to eat. The woman and her boy need our help, same as we have needed other folks' help. 'Freely ye have received, freely give.' So shall it be."

Tugging on Mother's skirt as it billowed out in front of her, Caroline suddenly thought of a way to help. "We could go to Anna's! Her father might know where to take the old man!"

"That's a fine idea, Caroline," Mother agreed. Turning to the Indian family, she said, "Shall I find a place for you to go rest and warm yourselves while we get help?"

"We have only one place we must find," the woman said.

Mother nodded. Continuing down the road, Mother, Joseph, and Caroline plodded through a sloping snowdrift in front of the wheelwright's shop, the woman and her son following behind. Mother said, "If Anna's father doesn't know where the boulders are, then we will have to send these people on their way, Caroline. I fear there's little else we can do for them."

Caroline didn't say a word. She was numb with cold and longed to be back in her frame house, but first she wanted the old man to find his resting place.

"And now it is *you* out in a terrible storm!" Mr. Short exclaimed as he pulled open the door and found Mother and Caroline standing there. "Come in, come in!"

"Thank you, Mr. Short," Mother said. They stepped inside.

"Some travelers have come to town searching for a place where a row of boulders and fir trees stands watch by running water. They've traveled far with an old man who has little time to live and wants to see this place one last time. They're waiting outside."

"Could it be along the creek that cuts right here through town and heads south toward the meadow?" Mr. Short wondered aloud. "I have my sled and the oxen. I can search up and down the creek faster than any of us could on foot."

"Thank you kindly." Mother gratefully relented. "My children are at home waiting for supper, and I'm afraid I've kept Caroline and

Joseph out far too long already."

"Of course, ma'am," Mr. Short said. "Just one minute while I get my coat and tell my Anna I'll be going."

"Will she be all right by herself?" Mother asked.

"Anna?" Mr. Short grinned. "She'll have the whole magazine Caroline kindly lent her read clear through by the time I return!"

Caroline visited with Anna until Mr. Short was all bundled up and ready to lead the travelers down the final path of their long journey. The travois and the old man trailed along slowly behind, bumping up and down on the snow-covered road.

"May the good Lord watch over you," Mother said with a final wave.

"Do you think they will find his resting place, Mother?" Caroline asked hopefully.

"I am certain of it," Mother said, sliding her arm beneath Caroline's. "By nightfall, the old man will be home."

MAPLE FROLIC

"Mr. Ben says the days are just now getting warm enough and the nights staying chilly enough for the sap to start running, Mother. He asked if we'd come help him and Charlie tap the trees," Henry announced one evening. "He said we had to ask you first, seeing how it means we'll have to miss some days of school."

"Mr. Ben says that if we can help, Mother, he'll gladly give us half of the first sap he collects," Joseph added. "So we'll get the best sugar, same as him. We can take some of the later sap home to make molasses, too," he added. "But Mr. Ben thought my telling you about the first sap would convince you to let us help him."

"And he's right." Mother smiled. "There's nothing I'd like more than some fresh maple sugar! You may help Mr. Ben for as long as he needs you, boys. But I expect you to spend your evenings learning the lessons you're missing in school instead of playing checkers. Spring's here, and your schooling's almost finished until after the harvest."

"Yes, ma'am," Joseph replied dutifully as Henry slapped his knee and shouted, "Yee-haw!"

Dragging heavy buckets across the forest and stirring kettles full of boiling sap over a blazing fire did not sound at all like something Caroline wanted to do. She didn't know what her brothers were so excited about.

Mother's eyes were shining, too. "When the boys bring home some fresh maple sugar, the rest of us will be busy, too," she said, very seriously.

"Busy?" Caroline asked, waiting for Mother to tell her what new chore they'd have to do.

"Getting ready for our very first Maple

Frolic, of course!" Mother said, her green eyes sparkling merrily.

"A Maple Frolic?" the girls asked simultaneously.

"Henrietta Stoddard is hosting one this year," Mother said excitedly. "Mrs. Stoddard's told me she's planning to wear the dress I made her for Christmas. There will be music, and dancing, and all the guests will bring their own maple-sugar desserts. And knowing Mrs. Stoddard, we can expect a magnificent feast."

Spreading out the folds of her own gray skirt, Caroline examined it closely. In a few places, the wool was almost worn through. Her dress had no lively print or color or interesting trim. Even Mother couldn't make this dress look pretty, Caroline decided, slumping in her seat.

"Don't worry, Caroline, we'll have perfectly fine dresses to wear," Mother assured her. "Not long ago we received some lovely material."

"In the Christmas trunk!" Martha exclaimed.

"Indeed!" Mother laughed. "I've already cut the material for each dress, and the boys' trousers won't take much more work. I just may be able to finish your party clothes in time for the celebration. I'll be so busy sewing, it'll be as if I owned my dress shop again!"

Martha jumped up from her chair. "We're going to a party!" she shouted.

"And we'll have new dresses!" Eliza gleefully clasped Martha's hands, and they spun around the room in circles.

"And buckets full of my favorite! Sugar syrup!" Caroline laughed, jumping up and down and joining the circle.

Setting her threaded needle and mending neatly on the sewing table, Mother stood up, smoothed her skirt, and extended her arms in a grand gesture. "You'll have to learn to do more than twirl and hop if you're to dance at such a fine party, children," she teased, gathering the sides of her skirt and swishing it from side to side. "I'll have to teach you every jig I can remember!"

Mother and the boys quickly carried the chairs away from the center of the room and slid the table out of the way. After arranging the children in a line from tallest to shortest,

Mother jigged to her place in front of them, slowly calling out steps as she danced them. The fire in the hearth squeaked and popped and danced along as the girls swayed, the boys bowed, Thomas ran in circles around the room, and Mother clapped and counted each step.

Watching Mother's graceful movements intently, Caroline tried to imitate her every step and gesture. But now and again her feet hopped where she didn't want them to go, and sometimes they got all mixed up with each other. Henry was in even worse shape than Caroline, crashing into the table and chairs on more than one occasion and shouting, "Swing your partners! Swing your partners!"

Mother curtsied one last time and fell breathless into her rocker, laughing with delight. "Enough!" She gasped. "You'll be a fine group of dancers in time for the Maple Frolic!"

Each morning for the next two weeks, Henry and Joseph left the house before daylight to help Mr. Carpenter and Charlie collect sap and make maple sugar. Mother worked tirelessly, measuring, stitching, cutting, and trimming the dresses. When Mother wasn't busy sewing, the girls would help her with tasting and sweetening the maple.

"It's just about ready," Mother said, dipping her wooden spoon into the dark sap bubbling gently on the stove. She slowly lifted a spoonful above the rim and tipped the spoon over. A smooth, shimmering stream of creamy liquid flowed back into the pot.

Turning to the children, who were hovering around the stove waiting patiently for a taste, Mother said, "It's time to make our maple sweet for the frolic! Boys, fill four buckets with the freshest, cleanest snow you can find. Martha, spoon some flour into a cup, please, and bring it over to the table."

"What can I do, Mother?" Caroline asked.

"You may come along with me to the cellar, Caroline, and pick out some sprigs of mint while I get the butter."

Mother pulled the heavy door up from the floor and they climbed into the dark cellar.

"The mint is over there with the other

herbs," Mother said, pointing to the farthest corner of the cellar. Dried herbs tied with fuzzy strands of twine hung upside down from the ceiling. "You need only pull one sprig. I just want to give the syrup a touch of the flavor."

Standing beneath the hanging herbs, Caroline looked up at the leafy bundles, wondering which one was the mint that Mother wanted. The leaves on every hanging plant were a grayish green color, and most of them were different shapes and sizes. Each tiny leaf had crinkled and curled into itself, and none of them looked like they belonged in a maple sweet.

"Is this one mint, Mother?" Caroline finally asked, pointing above her head.

"No, that's sorrel," Mother told her. "Count three more plants, Caroline: sweet woodruff, linum, sage. There! You're standing beneath the mint now. Smell it and see."

Reaching up, Caroline gently tugged a thin stalk until it came loose from the knotted twine. Caroline held the herb to her nose. "It smells sweet, Mother," she said between sniffs. "It must be the mint."

"Good," Mother replied. "I've got the brick of butter. Let's get back upstairs."

Pushing aside a curvy strand of hanging onions, Caroline climbed upstairs into the bright room. Two buckets of snow were waiting beside the door, and Joseph and Henry had already hurried back outside to get another two. Eliza sat waiting by the table, swinging her legs impatiently beneath her seat. Martha waited there as well, holding a tin cup of flour.

"We've got all the ingredients ready, thanks to my helpers." Mother smiled as she placed the butter on the table and turned toward the stove. "Now all we need is some maple syrup."

Mother scooped a dipperful of the thick syrup into a wide bowl and dropped a chunk of butter on top. When it melted into a creamy white puddle, Mother whipped the syrup and butter with a wooden spoon until it was blended, sprinkled a handful of flour over the top, and stirred the mixture again. Finally she said, "Now each of you take a mint leaf and crumble it into the bowl."

Caroline pulled a shriveled leaf from the

dried stem and passed the sprig along to Martha and Eliza. Peering into the bowl, she rubbed the leaf between her fingers and scattered the gray-green crumbs onto the syrup. After Martha and Eliza had tossed their mint into the bowl, Mother gave the mixture one final whipping and said, "It's ready to be chilled."

As Mother carried the buckets of snow to the table, Joseph and Henry came running back into the house with two more buckets, partially filled with snow and ice. Then they knelt beside the buckets and watched Mother drizzle thick bands of the syrupy mixture across the snow. She waited a few moments for the bands to chill and harden, then cut them into tiny squares and placed them on a flat tin.

"Oh please, may we have a taste now?" Eliza pleaded.

"You may each have one sweet square," Mother said, relenting. "But we'll save the rest for the party."

Caroline chose a square from the tin and bit into the soft, chewy candy. It was still cold and dewy on the bottom, and had a fresh, tangy taste that reminded Caroline of a red-and-white-striped candy stick. She hadn't thought there could be anything she liked better than sugar syrup poured over hotcakes, but suddenly she had a new favorite treat.

Just when Caroline thought she couldn't have any more fun, Mother said, "It's time to dress for the party."

One step in front of her sisters, Caroline raced to the top of the stairs and looked over at the bed where Mother had laid out their new clothes. Clasping her hands together joyfully, she gushed, "Martha, Eliza, look!"

The dresses lay on top of the quilt beside a pile of white cotton stockings and petticoats. All three dresses were made from the red fabric that had arrived in the Christmas trunk. The red cotton was woven in plaids, and Mother had trimmed each collar, sleeve, and hem with a delicate white lace that was detailed with diamond shapes and dots. Tiny white buttons fell in a perfectly straight line from the middle of the collar down to the bright red sash that hugged each waistline, and the skirts were full and flouncy. Caroline was certain that Mother had never made them prettier dresses.

The girls chatted and giggled as they pulled on their stockings and petticoats and helped each other into their new dresses. When all their buttons were buttoned and all their shoes were laced, they walked slowly down the stairs and waited for Mother. For a few moments, Caroline sat quietly, just as she knew a young lady was supposed to wait, but then she just couldn't help standing up and spinning around in front of the hearth, watching the folds of her lovely dress fan out in a whirling blur of red plaid.

"Caroline!" Mother's voice called out from across the room. "We aren't at the party yet!"

Caroline felt her dress fall around her legs as she stopped instantly, and turned to face Mother. "Oh, Mother!" she breathed. "You are so pretty!"

Mother was standing on the far side of the hearth, where the soft glow of firelight made her gold-colored dress shine richly. She had styled her hair so that it curved below her ears and gathered in a bun at the nape of her neck.

The curved neckline of Mother's dress fell just below the ringlets, and the shoulders of her sleeves puffed into perfect circles. The dress's simple bodice fit snugly to her waist, then flared out into a golden bell skirt. Caroline thought she looked just like an angel.

"All of our dresses are so perfect, Mother," Martha crowed. "There won't be any other girls at the party who will look nearly as fine!"

Henry bounded down the stairs that very moment with Joseph and Thomas close behind. The boys were wearing new navy blue trousers; clean, starched white shirts; and suspenders. They had even neatly parted and combed their hair.

"Put on your coats and shawls, children, and we'll be on our way," Mother said as she began to bundle up Thomas.

Caroline hated to cover her new dress with her old woolen shawl, but she didn't want to miss one single moment of the party, so she didn't complain. Wrapping the shawl around her shoulders, she followed her family out into the chilly March air.

She had often passed Mrs. Stoddard's magnificent home and always wondered what it looked like inside. Surrounded by maples and pines, the house was set back majestically from the road. It was two tall stories high with chimneys at either end and a shingled roof that angled upward to a steep point. Slender glass windows adorned all four sides, and Caroline could hardly keep herself from peeking through the front window that was set beside the great oak door.

When they finally got inside the house, Caroline couldn't believe her eyes. The parlor to her left was crowded with gentlemen wearing fine vests and boots and ladies dressed in their most elegant outfits. A stenciled pattern of wine-colored roses decorated the walls, and rich, velvety drapes framed every tall window and doorway. The mantel above the blazing hearth was filled with treasures: a wooden clock with gold hands, a china dove, and a pair of silver candlesticks. In a far corner of the room, a large piano gleamed, its ivory and ebony keys waiting to be played. Caroline had never imagined a scene so lovely.

"Mrs. Quiner! I am so happy to see you!" Mrs. Stoddard welcomed Mother and Caroline nearly jumped in surprise.

"Good day, Mrs. Stoddard," Mother said, and began to introduce her children one by one.

"Hello, dear," Mrs. Stoddard patted her hand when it was Caroline's turn to greet her hostess. "How lovely your dress is. I expect your mother made it for you?"

"Yes, ma'am," Caroline answered. "She made hers, mine, and my sisters', too! And all the boys' clothes!"

"She made my dress as well," Mrs. Stoddard confided. Her sparkly silver-white hair was neatly caught up in a bun, and she was wearing the rich, black dress trimmed with ivory lace that Mother had made.

"We should bring your dessert into the dining room and place it with the rest of the treats," Mrs. Stoddard said. "And then, how about a tour of the house?"

"Oh yes, please!" Caroline, Martha, and Eliza said eagerly.

Turning her attention to Henry, Joseph, and Thomas, Mrs. Stoddard said, "Boys, I do believe you'll find some of your friends in the parlor, if you're not interested in touring the house."

The boys thanked her, and disappeared.

Lifting her cane, Mrs. Stoddard walked slowly down a long hall and turned into a room that was as big as the parlor, and crowded with chairs, cabinets, and tables. Near the entrance to the room, two wooden dish dressers stood beside each other, grapevines and pears stenciled along their curvy tops and sides. Blue-and-white china bowls, plates, and serving dishes filled the shelves.

Moving closer for a better look, Caroline marveled at the tall buildings and stately homes painted on each plate and bowl. "What places are these?" she asked politely.

"That is the statehouse in Boston," Mother answered, looking over Caroline's shoulder.

"And the rest of the engravings are of Boston estates," Mrs. Stoddard added. "I packed all this china and brought it from my home in Massachusetts. My husband wanted to leave it behind, but I insisted it make the journey with us. The china has been in my family for some thirty years."

Next, Mrs. Stoddard led them to the opposite side of the room, to the two long tables that overflowed with delicacies: pork, duck, chicken, and venison; codfish and whitefish; baked beans and fruit stuffing; stewed squash and potatoes; pickled cucumbers; baked bread, fresh butter, and currant jam; dried blackberry and pumpkin pies; and tins piled high with cookies and maple treats. Mother added her sweet squares to the feast just as a great roar of laughter and applause burst from the parlor and the fiddler quickened his song. "The guests must have started dancing," Mrs. Stoddard said. "Shall we join them?"

"Oh yes," said Caroline, who had been practicing her dancing for weeks. Now in her beautiful dress, dancing was sure to be even more fun.

The parlor buzzed with conversation and whirled with color as ladies and gentlemen danced and clapped merrily, and children twirled along. "Look, the boys are over by the piano with the Carpenters," Mother said, waving to them. "Let's go join them."

"Come on over, Charlotte!" Mr. Carpenter bellowed from across the room. "I need three dancing partners, and only the most peart girls in red dresses and matching bows will do!"

The fiddle rejoiced as Caroline, Martha, and Eliza showed Mr. Carpenter the dance steps Mother had taught them. Henry, Charlie, and Joseph soon jigged onto the floor and Mr. Carpenter disappeared into the crowd, leaving the children spinning and swinging from partner to partner until the fiddle finished its song and the feast began.

"Save some room for dessert," Mother advised as Henry heaped food onto his plate and then added extra helpings onto Caroline's. "I'll eat whatever you don't, little Brownbraid," he promised as they sat down with the others. All the food was so delicious that Caroline left only three forkfuls of stuffing and a bite of bread for Henry to finish, but still had enough room for three of Mother's tiny sugar squares and a taste of every other dessert on the table besides.

Even as daylight faded outside the plush curtains, Caroline longed to stay at Mrs. Stoddard's house for just a little while longer, but Mother soon appeared in the doorway with Thomas sound asleep in her arms. It was time to go home.

"Thank you for having us, ma'am." She smiled at Mrs. Stoddard and wrapped her shawl around her shoulders.

"I do hope you enjoyed yourself and that you'll visit again soon, Caroline," Mrs. Stoddard said warmly.

"I hope so, too," Caroline said.

Twinkling stars cheered the blue-black sky as hazy, white moonlight glazed the earth. Caroline breathed in the cold night air, recalling every wonderful moment of Mrs. Stoddard's Frolic.

GAME OF GRACES

Pausing at the top of the steep hill above the schoolhouse, Caroline took a deep breath. "It looks the same," she said. It was summertime again, and the one-room school was still nestled amid swaying grasses and wildflowers at the far end of the meadow.

"What did you expect?" Martha asked crisply, tossing her braids behind her shoulders with two quick jerks of her head. "A new schoolhouse?"

Actually, Caroline was glad to see it was the same. She couldn't wait to get back to the schoolhouse and begin her new lessons. Miss

Morgan would be there to greet her and all the other students she hadn't seen through the long winter would be there, too.

Caroline hurried into the schoolhouse and found Anna inside. She had already chosen the best bench in the small room. Sunlight poured through the window beside her, brightening her mop of dark curls as she waited for Caroline and Martha to join her.

"May I? Sit?" A soft voice said from behind them.

Caroline turned at once toward the aisle. Elsa was standing there, looking through her long bangs and smiling shyly. "Of course, Elsa!"

"We're still waiting for Miss Morgan. She is not here yet." Anna spoke slowly to Elsa, who gratefully sat down beside Martha.

The benches soon filled with girls and boys of all ages. All the students waited impatiently for the schoolmistress to appear. The chatter in the room was so loud that Caroline could hardly hear Anna and Elsa, until the door to the schoolroom shut with a bang. Every head in the room turned to the door. A stranger was standing at the back of the room. He was almost as wide as he was tall, and as he passed Caroline's row, she couldn't help staring in awe at his immense belly. Stuffed into a crisp, white shirt and tucked beneath black suspenders, it stretched so far that Caroline was afraid the suspenders might snap.

"A good morning to you, students," he said in a deep voice. "My name is Mr. Speare. I am your new schoolmaster."

Caroline looked at Martha, then at Anna and Elsa. The look of horror on their faces mirrored her own.

"Excuse me, sir," an older girl with freckles bravely said. "What's happened to Miss Morgan?"

"She's married a fellow by name of Donald Jackson and moved on to Waukesha," Mr. Speare said. "But she has left behind a journal full of notes detailing your progress. Each of you shall continue your studies wherever it is that you left off with her. I will call you to the front of the room one by one, and discuss any notes Miss Morgan left pertaining to you."

Caroline studied the enormous man seated at the front of the room. His black hair was pasted down over his head, comb lines running through it. Stray black hairs sprang out in all directions from the furry eyebrows that nearly hid his small gray eyes. She searched the new schoolmaster's face, wondering if he would use the long wooden stick he had just placed beside a tall stack of books on the table.

By the time Mr. Speare finally called Caroline's name, she was nervous. Trembling, she walked to the front of the room.

"You are Caroline Quiner?" he asked.

"Yes, sir."

"Miss Morgan writes that you have just begun your first reader and have completed more than half of the lessons in your spelling book," he said.

"Yes, sir," Caroline replied.

"Good for you, young lady," Mr. Speare said with a nod, and sent Caroline back to her seat.

"What's he like?" Martha whispered as Caroline sat down.

"He's not awful," Caroline replied honestly.

"He's not awful *yet*, you mean!" Martha declared.

As soon as Caroline sat down, Mr. Speare dismissed the students with a gentle reminder. "Return to your seats punctually, please, one hour from now."

"How could Miss Morgan just up and leave like that, without telling anybody?" Caroline was first to ask as she and Martha, Anna, and Elsa found a shaded grassy spot near some of their schoolmates and sat down to eat dinner.

"I wish *I* could just up and leave," Martha grumbled. "I'd run as fast and as far from that schoolhouse as I could go!"

Anna opened her lunch tin. "I've got some bread, some cheese, and a cold piece of pork. Same as last night's supper," she announced. "What'd you bring?"

"Beans!" Elsa said proudly, as if she had been practicing the word all morning.

Martha pulled two crumbly yellow cakes out of her tin, handed one to Caroline, and tipped the tin upside down. "Nothing but cornmeal patties again," she complained.

"You and Caroline can share some of my dinner," Anna offered. "Papa always sends me to school with too much. If you don't help me, it'll all go to waste."

"She's right, you know." Martha looked defiantly at Caroline as she accepted a piece of pork from Anna.

"Thanks Anna!" Caroline said, biting into the chunk of cheese that Anna handed her.

"Would you like some, Elsa?" Anna offered.

Elsa was sitting quietly across from Caroline and Martha, eating her beans and listening to every word. "No thank you," she finally said, dropping her spoon into her now-empty tin pail. "Play!"

"Play what?" Caroline asked.

Elsa pointed to two girls standing with their backs to them a few feet away. The girls were whirling a hoop decorated with bright ribbons back and forth to each other with two slim canes. "Play!" she repeated eagerly.

"They're playing the game of Graces, I think," Anna said. "Papa saw the wands and hoop in the general store a few months back, but they were too expensive. Papa said he'd get a hoop from the cooper and make me a set of my own."

Caroline couldn't take her eyes off the hoop soaring from girl to girl in a whirl of color. Its streaming colored ribbons fluttered through the air like a rainbow with wings. "Mother has a whole basketful of scraps from all the shirts and dresses she's made," Caroline said. "I'm sure she'd give us one or two scraps to hang on the hoops if your dad gets them."

As the four girls intently watched the game, a crowd of their schoolmates gathered behind them. The ribboned hoop was flung from player to player, and twenty braided heads turned at exactly the same time to watch each toss.

Caroline's smile disappeared as she looked from the spinning hoop to the players' faces. She had been so enthralled by the colorful ribbons sailing through the air, she hadn't paid attention to the girls playing the game. They were the very same two girls who had snickered at Martha more than a year ago when she had gone to church and hadn't worn any shoes.

Caroline had defended her sister at the church and had stood by Martha in front of the schoolhouse weeks later as Martha had told the girls exactly what she thought of them.

"Their dresses are even prettier than their hoop." Caroline sighed.

"Well, when we're finished with our hoops, they will be even prettier than their dresses," Martha said determinedly.

As they waited in line to file back into their bench, the two girls in the matching dresses stepped up beside Anna. Caroline stared straight ahead, pretending not to notice them.

"If you like the hoop so much, you can see pictures of it in *The American Girl's Book.*"

One of the girls was addressing Caroline. "Or you can just get yourself one at the general store. That's where we got ours. They come special made, all wrapped in a package, and fly *much* better than the homemade kind."

"They don't cost much, either," Susannah, the second girl began.

"Much less than a pair of shoes," the first girl finished snidely.

Caroline felt sick to her stomach. Her cheeks flushed red with shame and anger, and her fingers closed into tight fists at her sides.

The room fell silent as Martha whirled around and shouted, "What makes you think we'd ever want your silly hoop, or *anything* that belongs to the likes of you?" Her face was red with fury and her eyes were flashing as she pushed her way beside Caroline and stepped in front of Susannah. "If I wasn't standing here in a schoolroom full of girls who are nicer than you in every single way, I'd spit on your pretty dresses and smash your fancy hoop right over my knee till it broke into little tiny pieces, the perfect-size pieces for folks as small-minded as you!"

"Who is it spewing such venom in my schoolhouse!" Mr. Speare's angry voice demanded from the front of the room. "Caroline Quiner! Is that you shouting like that?"

Caroline looked from her sister's shocked face to the girls' prim expressions and thin, terrible smiles. Turning to face the schoolmaster and all the students crowding the aisle in front of her, Caroline answered loudly, in the bravest voice she could muster, "Yes, I said it. I'm sorry, sir."

"She did not, Mr. Speare," Martha spoke up immediately. "I said every word. And I meant it, too."

"And who are you?" the schoolmaster questioned, his thick eyebrows raised in suspicion.

"Martha Quiner, sir," Martha answered. "Caroline's sister."

"This is most peculiar," Mr. Speare said. "Two of you taking the blame for the atrocious conduct of only one. I'll ask you, again, Miss Caroline Quiner. Were you the cause of this scene?"

Caroline stared straight ahead at the schoolmaster, watching him drum his fingers on the table beside the long wooden stick. She might not have shouted the words that caused the awful fuss in the classroom, but as she looked at their smug faces once more, she wished with all her heart that she had uttered every single word. "Yes, sir," Caroline answered firmly. "It's all my fault."

"Caroline!" Martha gasped.

"Well," Mr. Speare said. "It takes grit to tell such a truth in front of a whole schoolroom of people, so I shall not send you home. However," he continued, "I expect both you and your sister to remain in the schoolhouse after your lessons, Miss Quiner. You may not return home until every last inch of this schoolhouse is scrubbed clean."

"Yes, sir," Caroline said.

When class was dismissed, Anna addressed the schoolmaster in a soft but determined manner. "We'd like to stay and help. If we may, sir."

"I stay also," Elsa said slowly.

"Most peculiar," Mr. Speare said, shaking his head in surprise. "Miss Morgan left word that there were troublemakers in this schoolhouse, but none of your names was listed as such. Please close the door when you leave, young ladies. I shall see you in the morning."

Without speaking, the girls scrubbed the wooden benches, swept the wood-plank floors, and wiped Mr. Speare's slate board clean, before shutting the schoolhouse door behind them.

"My fingers stink like lye." Caroline grimaced as she and Martha waved good-bye to their friends and called out one final thank-you before heading off through the meadow.

"Maybe we can ask Henry and Joseph to start whittling away at a hoop and some sticks for us tonight," Martha said, trying to cheer Caroline up.

"No." Caroline paused. "I don't think that game is much fun after all."

Of course, Mother got word of their afternoon at the schoolhouse, but she didn't scold the girls. Instead, she told Joseph to trade for a hoop from the cooper, and later that night he and Henry sanded the hoop and whittled three perfect wands out of long, straight sticks. The very next morning Mother called the girls over to her sewing table the moment they had finished their chores. Lifting her basket full of scraps, she said, "Choose the brightest-colored ribbons and scraps of material you can find, girls. You'll have nothing less than the prettiest hoop in town."

CORDUROY BRIDGE

One day after school, Caroline convinced Martha to take the shortcut across the creek.

"Over the corduroy bridge?" Martha asked.

On the edge of town, the corduroy bridge cut across the marsh and the creek. It was made of a wide raft of logs that had been laid down carefully side by side. Caroline loved balancing on the logs, which shifted and rolled beneath her bare feet as she stepped from one to the next. "If we hurry, we'll get to cross over it two times and still make it home in time for supper!"

Knee-high grass and wildflowers bent this

way and that, tickling Caroline's bare legs as she ran along toward the creek. Wildflowers grew side by side with velvety brown cattails, and the scatterings of marsh milkweed tinted the wetlands a soft pink.

"What's that noise?" Martha asked.

Caroline stopped and listened. The still summer air was alive with the buzz of mosquitoes and flies. Muskrats rustled about as crickets chirruped, and the songs of red-winged blackbirds, perched about the cattails, lilted across the marsh. Beneath these sounds of summer, a tinny blast, followed by a thump and a rattle, grew louder and louder.

"I don't know what it is, but it's coming from the bridge, I think!" Caroline said.

Braids flying, Caroline and Martha dashed to the corduroy bridge.

"It's music!" Caroline called out to Martha in between breaths. "A fife like Anna's, and a bugle . . . and a drum, I think!"

"Two drums, at least!" Martha shouted back. "One boom's louder than the other."

As the rolling logs of the corduroy bridge

came into view, the music stopped. In the distance, Caroline could see a short line of people dressed in dark blue shirts and trousers crossing the bridge in single file. Plumed white feathers flounced out of their fiery red hats, and sashes cut diagonally across their shirts.

"It's a parade!" Caroline shouted.

"It must be a whole band! Keep going," Martha urged. "I want to see it up close."

As Caroline and Martha reached one side of the bridge, a great clattering shook the air, followed by the piercing blast of a bugle. Caroline and Martha watched as two sleek, black horses and a wide wagon rumbled up to the edge of the bridge. The horses set their shoes on the first log of the bridge tentatively, only to whinny loudly and step back onto solid ground.

"Git on with ya!" a man shrieked. "It's just a blasted bridge! And we've seven more miles to go 'fore we get to Waukesha! Git *on* with ya!"

With a cacophony of snorts, whinnies, and grunts from the horses and angry shouts from the driver, the horses and wagon finally bumped across the log bridge. "M-A-B-I-E," Caroline read the bold, black letters painted on the side of the wagon. They were followed by the letters C-I-R-C-U-S. Both words were framed in a big rectangle that was painted orange. "Martha, it's the Mabie Circus! I think it's just the beginning!" Caroline sang out. "Look! There are some funny-looking folks behind the horses!"

"Clowns!" Martha exclaimed. "I've seen them in town on posters for the circus!"

The first clown wore baggy gray trousers and a blousy white shirt that was dotted with enormous red spots. A pointed hat was slanted above his mop of curly black hair, and his face was painted white. The second figure was dressed in a shirt and multicolored trousers stitched together from rags. His face was rubbed black with charcoal, and only his painted white mouth was visible, a wide, shining grin that spread from ear to ear.

Caroline was so fascinated by the clowns, she hadn't even noticed that one was holding a small bundle all dressed up in a flowery print dress. She shrieked in surprise when the bundle began squirming in the clown's arms and poked a pink snout out of a fold in the dress. "It's a baby pig," Caroline said, giggling. "And it's wearing a bonnet!"

Turning his head toward the sound of the girls' laughter, the dotted clown waved at the girls with his other white-gloved hand.

"The clown sees us, Martha!" Caroline cried. "He's waving right at us!" Jumping up and down, Caroline waved back, laughing gleefully as the clown tried to balance across the rolling logs and wrestle with his squirmy pig at the same time.

Behind the clowns, a massive man with a tightly cropped beard was stepping up to the first log, towering over the two creamy white steeds that followed him. He wore a sleeveless green shirt that showed off his huge arms and rippling muscles. His long legs were as wide as tree trunks, and his boots looked as big as logs.

"He must be one of those giants Mother reads about in our storybooks," Caroline whispered.

Just then a rectangular cage with wooden

beams rattled and clanged toward the bridge. A big animal, all furry and white, was moving and twisting about inside the cage. "What is *that*?" Caroline asked, leaning forward for a better look.

The cage bumped and clattered over the logs, and when it was finally in full view, the animal inside flashed its furry white face, with its black nose and eyes, at Caroline and Martha. "It's a bear!" Martha exclaimed. "A white bear!"

"Whoever heard of a white bear?" Caroline asked, dumbfounded. In the forests around town, she had seen black bears from a distance, and brown bears, too. But never had she even heard of a white bear.

"Everyone who's ever seen a circus, I guess," Martha said.

A shrill, shrieking trumpet blared through the air. Caroline's stomach flipped, and she jumped backward in the grass. A second shriek followed as a great gray beast thumped toward the bridge in smooth, rhythmic strides, swinging its wrinkly gray trunk and flapping its immense gray ears. "An elephant!" Caroline and Martha shouted at once.

When the elephant arrived at the edge of the creek, it dipped its trunk into the tumbling, bubbly water and stood perfectly still. Rolling its long nose up to its mouth, it snorted and squirted all the water it had drawn from the creek inside.

"It's drinking!" Caroline laughed delightedly.

"Move along, old gal!" A thin man walking beside the elephant called out. Pushing up his green-and-gray flannel sleeves, the man led the enormous animal to the foot of the bridge.

The elephant stepped up to the first log and raised its huge leg. Placing its enormous foot down on the log, it shifted its weight, swinging its trunk and hesitating before moving forward onto the next log.

"It's afraid of the logs!" Martha said incredulously. "That big old elephant is afraid of a bridge made of logs!"

"It's tiptoeing, Martha!" Caroline cried, watching the elephant shuffle its huge gray toes from one log to the next. "An elephant that tiptoes!"

Caroline and Martha clapped and laughed and urged the elephant forward. They were still jumping up and down on the edge of the marsh when the great gray beast stepped off the bridge, trumpeted in victory, and trotted off with a resounding *thud, thud, thud* after the circus wagons.

Carts filled with cages occupied by playful monkeys and slithering snakes, rolled one after the other over the bridge. Caroline and Martha *ooh*ed and *aah*ed as each one passed. By the time the last wagon rolled off the bridge, Caroline's palms were red and stinging from clapping so much, and her throat felt raspy and sore.

"They must be heading straight through town if they're going to Waukesha," Martha said, reaching into the grass and gathering her books. "We can follow them till we get to the crossroads, and then we'll have to run the rest of the way home so we won't be late. I can't wait to tell everyone about the circus!"

Following Martha over the corduroy bridge, Caroline balanced from one log to the next on the soles of her bare feet, stepping in the footsteps of all the animals and circus folk who had crossed the bridge only moments before. She looked back at the corduroy bridge behind, thinking how glad she was that they'd taken the shortcut today.

White Bears

"If we fill both these buckets, Eliza, we'll have enough feed for Hog and we won't have to come back for more," Caroline explained as she followed Wolf across forest paths that were speckled with sunshine. "Pick all the beechnuts and hazelnuts and acorns you can find."

Each evening in summer and fall, Caroline and Martha spent the hour before supper in the woods, collecting buckets of nuts and berries to feed Hog. Caroline loved this chore, roaming through the forest, smelling the fresh evergreens, spying on the squirrels and rabbits scampering from sunspot to sunspot. Today

Caroline was teaching Eliza how to help.

The wooden bucket became heavier and heavier as Caroline tossed handfuls of nuts and berries inside. A little bit more and she would be done.

A rustling of leaves and two loud thuds followed by a yelp and a hoot suddenly broke the stillness of the hushed forest. Caroline jumped. "Eliza?" she called, looking all around her as Wolf's sharp barking resonated through the trees.

"I'm over here!" Pointing straight ahead, Eliza whispered, "I saw something, Caroline. Way down there."

At the very dimmest, farthest point of the forest, Caroline could just barely see a white figure bounding up a tree. The next instant, a second white figure followed the first. "Get your bucket and hurry, Eliza," Caroline said urgently. "We have to go now."

Pulling Eliza by the hand, Caroline dashed through the forest, skirting trees and stepping over twisted roots and vines that jutted up from the ground. Not once did she look back until she stepped into the soft meadow that was flooded with sunlight at the forest's edge. The climbing white figures were nowhere to be seen.

"They didn't follow us, I don't think," Caroline said breathlessly.

"Can we stop? Please!" Eliza panted.

"For a minute," Caroline agreed. Setting her bucket on the ground, she bent over and, hands on her knees, breathed fast and deep. She glanced into her bucket to see how many acorns and nuts she had lost on her trek out of the woods, relieved to find it was still almost full. "Eliza, where's your bucket?"

"The wood was digging into my fingers, and you were going so fast, and I let it go! Don't be mad," she pleaded, near tears. "We can go back and get it. We can fill it up again in no time."

"Not now we can't!" Caroline snapped. "I'm not going anywhere near that forest. Those were white bears in those trees!"

"White bears!" Eliza exclaimed. "How do you know?"

"I saw one when the circus passed through town last month. Whatever was climbing those trees was big and fast and white. What else could they be but white bears?"

Eliza scrambled to her feet. "I want to go home now," she said, her voice quavering.

"Me, too," Caroline said, reaching for her bucket.

Back home, Caroline took Hog's feed to the barn. It smelled sweet and dusty, and she took a deep breath, feeling safe again as she stepped around piles of hay; oats and barley, scattered about the dirt floor, stuck to her bare feet.

She was skipping back past the garden when a flash of white dashed by on the dirt road in front of the house. In a second, she was scared again, and she flew across the yard, burst through the door of the frame house, and slammed it shut behind her.

"For goodness' sakes!" Mother exclaimed. "What are you doing, Caroline, slamming that door like that?"

"I'm . . . I'm sorry, Mother," Caroline said, her hand pressed against her heaving chest. "I saw the white bears! They were running loose in front of the house!"

"Caroline Lake Quiner!" Mother said incredulously. "You've never been one to make up such stories! What has gotten into you, child?"

"It's not a story, Mother," Caroline cried. "Ask Eliza! We were in the woods getting food for Hog and we heard some noises and looked and saw two white bears climbing in the trees!"

"Is this true, Eliza?" Mother asked her youngest daughter, who was at the washstand scrubbing her hands.

"Yes, ma'am," Eliza answered, nodding her head emphatically. "We saw them. Two white bears."

Mother began peeling an onion. "All the days I've lived in Wisconsin, I have never yet heard a body tell a story about seeing a white bear," she said.

"I saw a white bear that day the circus passed over the corduroy bridge," Martha spoke up from the table she was busy setting. "Caroline saw it, too."

"A white bear in a cage, perhaps," Mother agreed. "But there aren't any running free in the forests, Martha. Whatever it was you saw,

Caroline," Mother firmly assured her, "it wasn't a white bear. I'm as certain of that as I am that the sun will rise in the morning."

"They weren't just in the woods, Mother," Caroline persisted. "When I was coming from the barn just now, I saw them running down the road right in front of our house!"

"How could you see anything in front of the house when you were all the way back at the barn?" Mother asked. "And the day just shy of twilight, no less. Your eyes were playing tricks on you, Caroline. Now wash up, and not another word about white bears. You're scaring your little sister, and your baby brother can surely hear your tale from the other room as well. I'll not have a pack of sleepless children under my roof tonight!"

Just before supper, Henry said to Caroline, "Hey, little Brownbraid, I just came from the barn. I think we're missing a bucket of feed for Hog. Did you and Eliza get two this afternoon?"

Caroline didn't want to get into trouble for talking about the white bears, but she didn't know what else to say. "It's still in the woods,

Henry," Caroline whispered, staring at the dirt floor as her cheeks grew hot with shame.

"In the woods?" Henry asked, tousling his already tousled hair. "I don't understand. Why collect a bucket of Hog's feed and leave it sitting in the woods?"

"Eliza left it," Caroline said. "It wasn't her fault. We were running out of the forest as fast as we could."

"Running?" Henry asked. "From what?"

Caroline's voice grew louder and her words tumbled out so quickly, Henry could barely understand what she was saying. "From the white bears!" she cried. "They got loose from the circus and were climbing some trees in the woods, and we saw them and ran as fast as we could to get away. They followed us all the way home!"

"Whoa!" Henry hollered, his forehead wrinkling with concern as he dropped his broom with a thud and took firm hold of his sister's shoulders. "Stop right there 'fore you make yourself sick, Caroline! Are you talking about the woods out back of Mrs. Stoddard's?"

Unable to speak, Caroline nodded her head.

"Right after school, before supper?" Henry questioned.

"Yes," Caroline squeaked out.

"Well, that story just doesn't make any sense," Henry said. "I was in that very same forest with Charlie just now. We were climbing all sorts of trees, and neither one of us saw any white bears!"

"I just saw them again right after I left Hog's bucket in the barn."

Henry looked at Caroline for a moment, his eyes puzzled. Suddenly the wrinkles on his brow disappeared, his eyes lit up, and he tossed his head back, yelping with laughter.

"What's so funny?" Caroline asked.

"The white bears!" Henry gulped for air. "Don't you see? The white bears were me and Charlie!"

"Don't you laugh at me, Henry Quiner," Caroline snapped.

"I'm not laughing at you. It was us! We were climbing trees and fooling around in those very same woods. We were the ones you saw running past the house, too!"

"You and Charlie don't look anything like white bears!" Caroline shouted back at her brother.

"We did," Henry answered. "We took off all our clothes, save our long underwear, so we wouldn't tear them when we were climbing in the trees."

"It was *you*?" Caroline asked, weak with relief.

"*I'm* your white bear, little Brownbraid." Henry grinned. "Me and Charlie, that is. Maybe we should join us a circus and dance around in our underwear!"

Finally, Caroline had to laugh. She'd been afraid of her very own brother.

Henry tugged on her braid and said, "Now that there's nothing to be afraid of, what do you say we get that lost bucket from the woods?"

LETTERS

Early one morning, the air outside the frame house pulsed with a low, steady rumble. Even before she looked out the window, Caroline knew the pigeons had arrived. The sky was suddenly darkened by millions of birds, flapping their wings and gliding together in an endless throng, flying south for the winter.

The pigeons would strip the woods, fields, and trees in Brookfield of the seeds, grain, berries, and wild nuts that hadn't yet been harvested, so each day Henry and Joseph spent hours with all the men and boys in town trapping and killing the pigeons.

On the final morning of the hunt, Henry was exuberant. "Mr. Ben says this is the finest haul he can remember," he exclaimed. "Mr. Carleton's paying top dollar for the pigeons. Two whole cents a bird! Do you know what that means, Mother?" Henry asked, his face glowing. "That means we're going to bring us home more than ten whole dollars!"

"I can think of many more pleasant ways to earn money than slaughtering all those birds," Mother remarked as she filled Thomas's cup with milk.

"But *ten* dollars, Mother!" Henry protested. "We made ten dollars. That's almost rich!"

Mother smiled. "You and Joseph have worked hard these last few days, and your father would have been proud of you."

"Thomas is proud, too!" Thomas grinned and pounded his little fist on the table.

"I don't understand how you can hunt so many birds all at once," Caroline admitted, spreading some butter on her hotcakes.

"It's not really like hunting," Joseph explained. "It's much easier because everywhere you look, you see pigeons. They're all over the forests and the meadows, eating whatever they find. We set traps with our nets to catch the birds, or sometimes we just step up behind them while they're eating and hit them with our sticks. This year, so many birds landed, we mostly just had to knock them dead out of the trees."

"Well, there will be plenty for us to pluck, then," Mother said. "We should begin first thing after our morning chores. I have a sack of goose feathers started that's not yet full enough to make into a pillow."

"For me!" Thomas said, his mouth full of hotcakes.

"Oh, one more thing, Mother," Henry said. "Last night Mr. Ben told me that Mrs. Carpenter told him that Mr. Porter told her that there's some letters come for you at the general store. I'm setting Hog loose in town this morning to fatten him up on bird carcasses—"

"Henry-O, we're eating," Mother warned.

"—and I could fetch your letters at the same time," Henry finished, his eyes lighting up.

"Kill two birds with one stone." He chuckled to himself at his joke.

"You'll have your hands full just keeping Hog in line, Henry-O," Mother said, thinking aloud. "Martha can begin the crust for the pigeon pie while Joseph, Eliza, and I pluck and clean the pigeons. That leaves Caroline to look after Thomas. They both can go along with you, Henry, and get the letters from the general store."

"You're going to let Caroline fetch something so important, Mother?" Martha asked.

"Caroline knows the value of a letter, Martha," Mother said dryly. "I expect she'll have little trouble in picking them up and bringing them home safely. Am I correct, Caroline?"

"Yes, ma'am." Caroline nodded importantly, with a sideways glance at Martha. "I'll be very careful."

As soon as the frame house was swept and tidied, Caroline took hold of Thomas's hand.

The cool morning breeze blew the folds of her apron across her brown woolen skirt as she stepped out of the house. "Seems the pigeons have gone away just as quick and sudden as they came," she said, looking at the clear blue sky.

"Where'd they go?" Thomas asked.

"Mother says they go south this time of year," Caroline answered.

"This way, Hog, move it!" Henry was shouting as he ran around the side of the house, Wolf trotting along behind. "Let's go." He waved to his brother and sister.

Caroline, Thomas, and Wolf crunched along the leaf-covered road behind Henry and their enormous pig. Holding Thomas's fingers tightly, Caroline giggled at the sight of Hog's wrinkled, fleshy backside waddling here and there while Henry tried to hurry him along.

As they neared the crossroads of town, the road suddenly grew crowded with men and boys driving their hogs toward the pigeon remains scattered about and tossed in heaps at the sides of wagons.

"They're eating up the birds!" Thomas exclaimed in wonder, pointing at the enormous pigs chewing dead birds all around him.

Feeling queasy, Caroline looked at Henry.

"I'm going for Mother's letters now."

"Watch your step," Henry said as he prodded Hog along.

For the first time that morning, Caroline wished she had stayed at home to pluck pigeon feathers instead of going to town. She held her breath and hurried Thomas through the littered, smelly road and into the general store.

"Well, good morning to you, Miss Quiner!" the storekeeper greeted Caroline as she closed the door behind her with a great sigh of relief and breathed in all the spices. "And to you, too, lad," he added, nodding his shiny bald head at Thomas.

"Good morning, Mr. Porter." Caroline tipped up her face to address the tall man. "Mother sent us to fetch some letters for her, sir."

"Ah, yes." Mr. Porter smiled. "One came a few days ago, I believe, and one arrived just yesterday. Here you are, young lady." He slid two thin, brown envelopes over the edge of the crowded counter. "It looks like the one on top has traveled all the way from back East."

"Thank you, sir," Caroline said excitedly,

examining the sprawling, black script on the top envelope. The letters were curvy and connected, and she couldn't read one word.

"Send my greetings to your Mother." Mr. Porter smiled down at her.

"I will," Caroline promised. "Thank you, sir, and good-bye."

"'Bye!" Thomas echoed.

Hog was still busily feasting when Caroline and Thomas ran up to Henry. "Here they are," she exclaimed, waving the letters in front of him. "Mr. Porter says one of them's from back East, but I can't make sense of any of the words on it."

"Bring it on home, Caroline," Henry said. "No sense in my taking Hog away from all this food. Tell Mother I'll be along by dinner."

Caroline couldn't wait to get home and learn more about the mysterious letters. Thomas hurried along behind her, trying to keep up. When they arrived at the frame house, Mother was placing the top crust over a pigeon pie. "Goodness, Thomas, your cheeks are as round and red as apples!"

"Caroline goes fast," Thomas complained.

"Did you get the letters?" Mother asked.

"Yes, Mother." Caroline smiled proudly. "They're right here, safe and sound! Mr. Porter says this one is from back East," Caroline said as she handed it to Mother. "And here's the other letter, too."

"He's right," Mother said, scanning the writing on the first envelope. "But it's not from Boston. I only hope it isn't . . ."

Sliding a knife through the edge of the envelope, Mother pulled out a single sheet of paper. Her eyes darted from one line to the next, and as she read, she slowly lifted her fingertips to her trembling lips, and her face grew terribly troubled.

"Please, Mother," Caroline asked as fear crept up inside her. "What's happened?"

"Oh, Caroline!" Mother said, her voice breaking as she folded the letter and stuffed it back into the envelope. "You mustn't worry." She tried to smile down at Caroline as she wiped the corners of her eyes. "It's not a matter that concerns you at this time. So run along to the barn and see if Joseph and Martha have finished with the pigeons."

Caroline knew she shouldn't ask any more questions, but Mother had the very same look of fear and worry on her face that Caroline had seen only once before, the day Uncle Elisha had arrived with news about Father's shipwreck. "Yes, ma'am," Caroline said, feeling sicker now than she had this morning about the pigeons.

Caroline hardly spoke during supper, and remained quiet as she embroidered at the sewing table with Mother and her sisters in the evening hour before bedtime. She knew Mother would tell them the news when the time was right.

Martha hummed as she clicked her knitting needles together, and Eliza carefully watched Mother's expert stitches so she could later practice similar stitches on her own piece of linen.

Joseph was stoking the fire, and Henry was sitting cross-legged on the floor in front of the hearth, whistling as he whittled away at a block of wood.

Suddenly Martha stopped humming. "Who were the letters from today, Mother?" she asked. "You never told us at supper."

Caroline studied the verse she was stitching on her sampler. She was too nervous to look up. She was the only one who knew the news might be bad.

"One was from Pennsylvania," Mother answered. "From a man named Michael Woods. It wasn't good news."

Joseph stopped poking the fire and turned away from the hearth. "What's happened, Mother?"

Setting down her needle and fabric, Mother glanced around the room at each expectant face. In a calm and steady voice, she recounted the contents of the letter. "Years ago," Mother began, "your father and I fell on some very hard times. We were forced to sell our land, and a friend of Father's, Mr. Michael Woods, who lived here in Brookfield, bought it. Mr. Woods didn't have any intention of living on the land, so he kindly let us remain here for a small amount of money. Even after he and his wife moved back to Pennsylvania, Mr. Woods never asked us to leave, but your father and I knew he'd want to reclaim the property someday for himself or his kin. Now his sister and her family are coming to Brookfield this spring. They plan to live on this land. We'll have to find another place to live."

"You mean we have to go away from here?" Martha asked, dropping her knitting needles on her lap as Mother finished her tale.

"Yes, Martha," Mother said. "And I don't yet know where we'll go. I have saved some money to buy land, but if we choose to purchase it from someone hereabouts, we'll likely get too little to farm and raise animals. We may need to go farther west. Land will be cheaper there."

Caroline dropped her head. She thought about Anna and Elsa, about the Carpenters, and about Mrs. Stoddard. Her thoughts raced as she imagined the little white church that Father had helped build, the shelves she loved to explore in the general store, the bubbling creek where she had collected buckets of berries and wildflower bouquets. She imagined the barn that had been her very first home, her bedroom and all the small, cozy rooms of their little frame house. Shutting her eyes as tightly as she could, Caroline tried to think and understand, but all she could do was cry.

"There's the money we made from the pigeons, Mother," Joseph said. "Mr. Carleton owes us ten dollars and fifty-six cents. It could help buy more land."

"You bet!" Henry agreed.

"Thank you, boys," Mother said.

"I don't have money," Thomas burst out from the settle, where he was stacking his wooden blocks.

"Well, I don't have much, either." Mother laughed. "So wherever we go, it will have to be a place where we can get a fair amount of land for a good price."

"When will we go?" Eliza asked, uncertain if Mother's news was good or bad.

"In the spring," Mother replied. "I hope to get us settled soon after the sap starts to flow, Eliza. But enough questions, children!" Mother lightened her tone, trying to be cheerful. "And enough of the glum faces. We should think of this as an adventure. A chance to start over with our own land, land that can't be taken away.

"And now I do have some happier news. The other letter was from Grandma. She writes that if all goes as planned, she and Uncle Elisha's family are coming to stay with us for Christmas Eve and Christmas Day!"

"Grandma!" Caroline exclaimed. She had all but forgotten the second letter the storekeeper had given her, but now that letter was bringing her the happiest news of the day. Caroline decided to wait to worry about leaving their house. For now, she was just going to look forward to Grandma coming back for Christmas!

SANTECLAUS

The fire in the hearth blazed and popped mightily on Christmas Eve, warming the little frame house and adding a smoky aroma to the delicious scents of the gingerbread, spice cookies, and crusty brown bread that Mother had baked. Caroline rubbed a small circle of frost from the windowpane and peeked out. The world was still beneath its white winter cloak. Nothing was visible except the round, fluffy snowflakes that fell heavily from the gray winter sky.

"Do you think Uncle Elisha will still come in all this snow?" Caroline asked Eliza as her little sister squeezed in beside her.

"I hope so," Eliza said.

The door flew open, and a huge oak log, caked with snow and chunks of ice, rolled into the room. Joseph and Henry followed, pushing both ends of the log across the room with their snowy boots. "Here it is, Mother," Henry cried. "Is it big enough?"

"It looks like it's big enough to burn for the full twelve days of Christmas." Mother laughed. "Good work, boys! Shut the door and try not to make too much of a mess getting it to the hearth."

"Surely you wouldn't close the door on a man bearing gifts!" Mr. Carpenter called out, poking his grinning face through the open door.

"Mr. Ben!" a chorus of voices greeted him as he stomped into the house.

"Christmas greetings to you all," Mr. Carpenter said. "Sarah's sent me out with the plum pudding." He placed a large, heavy bowl on the table.

"One of our favorite Christmas traditions!" Mother said graciously. "Thank you,

Benjamin. And Sarah, too."

Tugging on Mr. Ben's trousers, Eliza asked quietly, "Will you still bring Christmas pudding to our new house, Mr. Ben?"

"What new house is that?" Mr. Carpenter asked, kneeling in front of Eliza.

Trying to keep her smile bright, Mother told him the news. "Forgive me for not telling you and Sarah sooner."

"Me and the Mrs. have plenty of land just down the road, Charlotte," Mr. Carpenter said without pause. "We could easily build another house on it, and build it far enough from our'n that we'd never have to bother each other. Unless we wanted to, of course."

"Thank you, Benjamin," Mother said. "But who knows how long you and Sarah will stay here? We need to put down roots on our own land."

Mr. Carpenter nodded. "So where to, then?"

"I don't know yet," Mother admitted. "Somewhere we can get enough land to raise crops and livestock and keep the family eating. The boys are old enough to help care for such a place now. Since we don't have a lot of money, I imagine we will have to go farther west."

"I'll look into what's available, if you like, Charlotte," he offered kindly. "Maybe we can somehow keep the Quiners close to Brookfield. I know your neighbors would like nothing more!"

For the first time in months, Caroline felt better. Mr. Ben knew their secret now, and maybe he would help them find a place to live that wasn't so far away.

The merry jingle of sleigh bells tinkled outside the frame house. Caroline dashed to the window and rubbed her peephole clear of frost again. "It's a bobsled, Mother!" she cried. "It's Grandma and Uncle Elisha!"

And with that, Mr. Carpenter bade them Merry Christmas and left the frame house, giving a loud, cheerful greeting to the visitors, who were making their way inside.

"Grandma!"

"Dear Caroline," Grandma said, hugging her close. "How good to be home with you again."

Caroline nodded, holding Grandma tight

and feeling Christmas happiness fill her up.

Uncle Elisha and his wife were standing by the door, surrounded by Caroline's cousins William, George Henry, and John. Mother and Martha quickly took the bowls and platters that Uncle Elisha was balancing in his arms and set them on the table. The boys dropped their coats, stomped the snow off their boots, and ran to the hearth to begin their checkers matches with Henry and Joseph.

"How wonderful to see you all again!" Mother's eyes twinkled. "Mother Quiner, welcome back!"

The table was suddenly crowded with bowls and platters and crocks. "Did you ever imagine so much food?" Martha asked incredulously. "On our table?"

"Shortbreads and stuffing, Grandma's sweet potatoes and baked apples." Caroline pointed from platter to bowl. "Mince pie and plum pudding, Mother's Christmas bread, and a goose!" she exclaimed. "A whole big wonderful goose!"

"Three big wonderful geese!" Uncle Elisha laughed from behind them. "We brought along two more for your mother to store in the cellar. They'll be a nice treat in the winter months."

"Yes, sir, thank you," Caroline said politely as she turned to face her uncle. He was smiling down at her, and as she looked at him, Caroline noticed for the first time that Uncle Elisha looked like Father. His brown hair was dusted with gray and was much shorter than Father's, his eyes were dark brown instead of blue, and he had a neatly trimmed mustache that curled at the tips instead of the cropped beard and mustache that Father had always worn. And yet when he laughed, his cheeks flushed a bright red and his eyes crinkled up at the corners, just like Father's.

"I'm so pleased to see you again, Caroline and Martha," Uncle Elisha was saying. "You've grown up just fine! Your father would have been very proud of you."

"Thank you, Uncle Elisha," Caroline and Martha said.

"Elisha," Grandma called gently, "Charlotte has something she'd like to speak with you about. Come along now, girls. Mother says we must set the table for dinner."

"I'll be back in a moment," Uncle Elisha said with a wink.

"He's nice, I think," Caroline said reluctantly as she crossed to the dishstand with Martha. "I never liked him before," she admitted.

"That's only because he always came at the awfulest times," Martha said. "I like him now, too. I just wish he had some girls to bring to our house instead of all those boys."

As Grandma cleared all the food that was to wait for Christmas Day dinner, Caroline began setting the table.

Mother's voice resounded firmly from the corner of the room behind Caroline. "Of course it's a fine idea, but I'm afraid it would be far too costly to move the family to Milwaukee, Elisha."

With wide eyes, Caroline listened to every word of Mother's conversation, though she knew she shouldn't.

"But what alternatives do you have, Charlotte?" Uncle Elisha asked. "The children will be near family, at least. You can work at your craft, and need stay with us only until you have saved enough money to buy land nearby."

"You're more than kind to offer, but I am determined to buy our own homestead as soon as possible," Mother said resolutely.

"Our newspaper lists public works sales whenever they become public. In fact, if I'm not mistaken, there's about to be a sale in Jefferson County. It's not quite thirty miles from here, I believe," Uncle Elisha said.

"Please, Elisha," Mother urged, "send me the information as soon as you return to Milwaukee."

"My pleasure, Charlotte," Uncle Elisha said. "That, and anything else you need."

Caroline met Martha's eyes across the table.

"Why such a sad face?" Grandma asked as she came up beside Caroline and placed a small crock of butter in the center of the table.

"Oh, Grandma," she said softly, holding back tears, "I don't want to leave our house. I don't want to leave Anna and Elsa, Mr. Ben and the schoolhouse, the barn and the church. . . ."

Grandma pulled Caroline close against her, gently stroking her hair. "You must never be afraid to journey to new places, Caroline," she said. "Just think, had Mother stayed in Boston, she would never have met your father. Change is good for the soul and the heart. And in every new place, we meet new friends and have new experiences, without ever losing those we left behind. Do you understand?"

"I think so."

The family soon gathered around the table to eat and exchange tale after tale of Christmases past. Caroline remained quiet, considering Grandma's wise words. It would be awful to leave Anna and Mr. Ben, and all the familiar faces, places, and sights in this town she had called home for as long as she could remember. And yet somewhere, there were new friends just waiting to be met.

"We must soon be off to bed," Uncle Elisha announced, "if Santeclaus is to have any time to visit us before daybreak."

"Who?" Eliza asked, stifling a yawn.

"Who?" Uncle Elisha repeated in surprise. "You mean to say that you've never heard of Santeclaus?"

"No, sir," a chorus of voices answered.

"Well, then, I must tell you about old Santeclaus!" he said in his deep, gentle voice, dropping his harmonica into his pocket as Caroline and her sisters and brothers gathered around. "The tale goes something like this," he began.

> *"Old Santeclaus with much delight*
> *His reindeer drives this frosty night*
> *O'er chimney tops and tracks of snow*
> *To bring his yearly gifts to you.*

> *"The steady friend of virtuous youth,*
> *The friend of duty and of truth,*
> *Each Christmas Eve he joys to come*
> *Where love and peace have made their home."*

"What does Sant-e-claus look like?" Caroline asked, speaking the strange name slowly.

"Well, he's a plump, bearded fellow who

wears a long, red cape that's lined with white fur, and he carries an enormous sack on his back that's overflowing with presents. Now, I think that each of us should hang a stocking on the mantel and hurry off to bed. Then Santeclaus may still have time to visit once we're asleep, and fill every one of our stockings with a Christmas surprise."

Nine empty woolen stockings soon dangled above the sputtering fire. With warm hugs and good-night wishes, William, George Henry, and John climbed into the daybed and trundle downstairs, while Caroline followed her brothers and sisters upstairs to their room, sneaking one last glance at the stockings hanging above the hearth.

The frame house was soon quiet, and all the children were in bed. Closing her eyes, Caroline remembered every moment of this happy Christmas Eve and imagined the joyous Christmas Day that would follow. She thought about Grandma and about Uncle Elisha, who reminded her so much of her beloved father. She thought about leaving Brookfield and all her friends, but her thoughts kept turning back to the stockings hanging over the hearth, and this jolly man named Santeclaus.

Footsteps tapped softly on the stairs. Caroline turned her capped head toward the railing, and in the dim light, she could barely see Mother's face. "It's bitterly cold tonight," Mother whispered. "Keep yourself tucked in."

"Yes ma'am," Caroline whispered back.

"Good night now, Caroline." She turned to go downstairs.

"Mother?" Caroline called softly into the darkness.

"Yes?" Mother turned back.

"Do you think Santeclaus will come to our house tonight?"

"Yes, I think he will."

"And will he be able to find us again if we have to leave our house and go to a new one?"

Mother climbed the last two stairs and knelt down beside the girls' bed. "Uncle Elisha told us that Santeclaus likes to come where love and peace have made their home, did he not?"

"Yes." Caroline nodded.

"Then have no doubt, Caroline," Mother said, her smile glowing in the darkness. "Santeclaus will find our home wherever we may go."

Snuggling closer to Eliza as Mother's footsteps echoed down the stairs, Caroline closed her eyes and sighed happily. She knew Grandma and Mother were right. Home wasn't a house or a town, a barn or a church, or even the kindest of friends. Home was where her sisters breathed softly in slumber beside her and her brothers rustled their straw mattress as they twisted and turned in their sleep. Home was where Mother's soft, soothing melodies floated to the rafters. It didn't matter where they moved or settled, or what place they called home. Caroline finally understood. Home was anywhere she happened to live with the people she loved most.

CAROLINE'S ADVENTURES CONTINUE IN

LITTLE CLEARING
IN THE WOODS
by MARIA D. WILKES

GOOD-BYES

U ncle Elisha's wagon was packed and ready to go. Caroline was about to climb up and join her sisters, Martha and Eliza, when she suddenly whirled around.

"Wait!" she exclaimed. "What about my chickens?"

She dashed the short distance across the cold, dewy grass to Mr. Carpenter's wagon, where her brothers, Joseph and Henry, and their neighbors Benjamin Carpenter and his son, Charlie, were loading the Quiners' belongings into Mr. Carpenter's wagon. "Henry," she cried out breathlessly, "don't forget the hens!"

"Every one of them squawkers is packed already," Henry called out as he swung a hay-filled mattress over the side of Mr. Carpenter's wagon. "Any empty space left up there, Joseph?"

Joseph surveyed the sacks, barrels, tables, and trunks piled in front of him. Two reed hampers, tightly packed with clothes, were tucked between Mother's butter churn and the three large barrels that held salt pork, flour, and corn meal. A washtub rested in the center of the wagon, cradling a collection of iron kettles and the leftover beans, peas, and potatoes from last fall's harvest. Beside the tub, four wooden chairs rested upside down on top of a square oak table.

"Not hardly," Joseph said.

"You didn't pile anything on the hens, did you?" Caroline asked as she stepped up beside Henry and peered inside the wagon. "They won't like it one bit."

"If you think I want to find a gunny sack full of dead chickens when we get to Concord, you're mighty mistaken, little Brownbraid,"

Henry said, rolling his eyes. "Those chickens will be the only food we'll have to eat for weeks!"

"Don't say that!" Caroline cried. Ever since she was four years old, she had cared for the family's hens, collecting their eggs each morning, feeding them, cleaning out their henhouse, even naming them. She knew they weren't pets, but she still hated to think about eating them. "And don't call me little Brownbraid, Henry! I'm not little anymore!"

"Nine years old doesn't make you a grownup," Henry teased. "Now get back to Uncle Elisha's wagon, Caroline. We're 'bout ready to go."

LITTLE HOUSE · BIG ADVENTURE

LITTLE HOUSE IN THE BIG WOODS

FARMER BOY

LITTLE HOUSE ON THE PRAIRIE

ON THE BANKS OF PLUM CREEK

BY THE SHORES OF SILVER LAKE

THE LONG WINTER

LITTLE TOWN ON THE PRAIRIE

THESE HAPPY GOLDEN YEARS

THE FIRST FOUR YEARS

THE MARTHA YEARS

LITTLE HOUSE IN THE HIGHLANDS
MELISSA WILEY

THE FAR SIDE OF THE LOCH
MELISSA WILEY

THE CHARLOTTE YEARS

LITTLE HOUSE BY BOSTON BAY
MELISSA WILEY

ON TIDE MILL LANE
MELISSA WILEY

THE CAROLINE YEARS

LITTLE HOUSE IN BROOKFIELD
MARIA D. WILKES

LITTLE TOWN AT THE CROSSROADS
MARIA D. WILKES

THE ROSE YEARS

LITTLE HOUSE ON ROCKY RIDGE
ROGER LEA MacBRIDE

LITTLE FARM IN THE OZARKS
ROGER LEA MacBRIDE